Mitch Albom

The Five People You Meet in Heaven

Annotations by
Cornelia Kaminski

Ernst Klett Sprachen
Stuttgart

1. Auflage 1 13 12 11 10 9 | 2020 19 18 17 16

Alle Drucke dieser Auflage sind unverändert und können im Unterricht nebeneinander verwendet werden. Die letzte Zahl bezeichnet das Jahr dieses Druckes.

Internetadresse: www.klett-sprachen.de

Redaktion / Klett Editor: Paul Newcomb
Druck und Bindung: Print Consult GmbH, München
Umschlagfoto: MEV, Augsburg
Printed in Slovakia

ISBN 978-3-12-578192-4

9 783125 781924

CONTENTS

Additional Materials

Abbreviations used in annotations:

AE	American English
BE	British English
derog	derogatory
esp	especially
i.e.	id est (that is)
inf	informal
sb	somebody
sth	something
usu	usually
USA	United States of America
vulg	vulgar

About the author

Mitch Albom is the author of nine books and a full-time writer. His first work, *Tuesdays With Morrie,* (1997) a moving record of time spent with a close friend, a college professor who was dying, was an extremely successful memoir. Later he wrote a dramatised version for the theatre. He has also written numerous other plays and comedies which have been performed across the U.S. Further talents include being an award-winning journalist and radio host.

Albom has founded several charities to do with the arts, children and homeless people in the Detroit area where he lives. His most recent charity, "S.A.Y Detroit," is an umbrella program which funds shelters and cares for the homeless. He also raises money for literacy projects through a variety of means including his performances with *The Rock Bottom Remainders* (he plays the keyboards), a rock band made up of writers. In 1999 Albom was named National Hospice Organization's Man of the Year.

About the novel

The Five People You Meet in Heaven, first published in 2003, is the most successful U.S. hardback first novel ever. It tells the inspirational tale of an elderly amusement park worker who dies thinking his life on earth was meaningless and empty. "Eddie" is killed trying to save the life of a little girl during a tragic ride accident. He wakes up in heaven to learn that the first stage involves meeting five people who were affected by your life, some of whom you might know, some you might not. Eddie's "journey" through his life and the people he touched opens his eyes to how we are all interconnected with other peoples' lives. Praised by critics as "A powerful book" (*Time Magazine*) "Transcendent" (*Atlanta Constitution*) and "A book with the genuine power to stir and comfort its readers" (*The New York Times*), the novel has sold more than 8 million copies worldwide.

The TV movie of *The Five People You Meet in Heaven,* to which Albom wrote the screenplay, was first aired in the U.S. in December 2004.

This book is dedicated to Edward Beitchman, my beloved uncle, who gave me my first concept of heaven. Every year, around the Thanksgiving table, he spoke of a night in the hospital when he awoke to see the souls of his departed loved ones sitting on the edge of the bed, waiting for him. I never forgot that story. And I never forgot him.

Everyone has an idea of heaven, as do most religions, and they should all be respected. The version represented here is only a guess, a wish, in some ways, that my uncle, and others like him—people who felt unimportant here on earth—realize, finally, how much they mattered and how they were loved.

1 **dedicated to** written for – 4 **departed** dead, deceased – 10 **how much they mattered** how important they were

The End

This is a story about a man named Eddie and it begins at the end, with Eddie dying in the sun. It might seem strange to start a story with an ending. But all endings are also beginnings. We just don't know it at the time.

The last hour of Eddie's life was spent, like most of the others, at Ruby Pier, an amusement park by a great gray ocean. The park had the usual attractions, a boardwalk, a Ferris wheel, roller coasters, bumper cars, a taffy stand, and an arcade where you could shoot streams of water into a clown's mouth. It also had a big new ride called Freddy's Free Fall, and this would be where Eddie would be killed, in an accident that would make newspapers around the state.

At the time of his death, Eddie was a squat, white-haired old man, with a short neck, a barrel chest, thick forearms, and a faded army tattoo on his right shoulder. His legs were thin and veined now, and his left knee, wounded in the war, was ruined by arthritis. He used a cane to get around. His face was broad and craggy from the sun, with salty whiskers and a lower jaw that protruded slightly, making him look prouder than he felt. He kept a cigarette behind his left ear and a ring of keys hooked to his belt. He wore rubber-soled shoes. He wore an old linen cap. His pale brown uniform suggested a workingman, and a workingman he was.

Eddie's job was "maintaining" the rides, which really meant keeping them safe. Every afternoon, he walked the park, checking on each attraction, from the Tilt-A-Whirl to the Pipeline Plunge. He looked for broken boards, loose bolts, worn-out steel. Sometimes he would stop, his eyes glazing over, and people walking past thought something was wrong. But he was listening, that's all. After all these years he could *hear* trouble, he said, in the spits and stutters and thrumming of the equipment.

7 **boardwalk** *BE:* ['bɔ:dwɔ:k]; *AE:* ['bɔ:dwa:k] wooden construction which starts on the beach and goes over the water (here: the sea) – 7 **Ferris wheel** *Riesenrad* – 8 **taffy stand** small shop on the boardwalk, on which a special kind of sweet, soft candy ("taffy") is made and sold – 13 **squat** *BE:* [skwɒt]; *AE:* [skwɑ:t] small and well (athletically) built – 17 **cane** thin walking stick – 18 **craggy** uneven, not smooth – 28 **glazing over** becoming unclear and empty

With fifty minutes left on earth, Eddie took his last walk along Ruby Pier. He passed an elderly couple.

"Folks," he mumbled, touching his cap.

They nodded politely. Customers knew Eddie. At least the regular ones did. They saw him summer after summer, one of those faces you associate with a place. His work shirt had a patch on the chest that read EDDIE above the word MAINTENANCE, and sometimes they would say, "Hiya, Eddie Maintenance," although he never thought that was funny.

Today, it so happened, was Eddie's birthday, his 83rd. A doctor, last week, had told him he had shingles. Shingles? Eddie didn't even know what they were. Once, he had been strong enough to lift a carousel horse in each arm. That was a long time ago.

"Eddie!"... "take me, Eddie!"... "Take me!"

Forty minutes until his death. Eddie made his way to the front of the roller coaster line. He rode every attraction at least once a week, to be certain the brakes and steering were solid. Today was coaster day—the "Ghoster Coaster" they called this one—and the kids who knew Eddie yelled to get in the cart with him.

Children liked Eddie. Not teenagers. Teenagers gave him headaches. Over the years, Eddie figured he'd seen every sort of do-nothing, snarl-at-you teenager there was. But children were different. Children looked at Eddie—who, with his protruding lower jaw, always seemed to be grinning, like a dolphin—and they trusted him. They drew in like cold hands to a fire. They hugged his leg. They played with his keys. Eddie mostly grunted, never saying much. He figured it was because he didn't say much that they liked him.

Now Eddie tapped two little boys with backward baseball caps. They raced to the cart and tumbled in. Eddie handed his cane to the ride attendant and slowly lowered himself between the two.

"Here we go. ...*Here we go!...*" one boy squealed, as the other pulled Eddie's arm around his shoulder. Eddie lowered the lap bar and *clack-clack-clack,* up they went.

3 **to mumble** to talk quietly and indistinctly – 7 **maintenance** ['meɪntənənts] activity that involves keeping something in good working order – 11 **shingles** herpes *(Zoster)* – 22 **to snarl at sb** to address sb in an angry, aggressive tone – 23 **to protrude** to stick out – 26 **to hug** to squeeze tightly in your arms – 26 **to grunt** to make a low, animal-like noise

A story went around about Eddie. When he was a boy, growing up by this very same pier, he got in an alley fight. Five kids from Pitkin Avenue had cornered his brother, Joe, and were about to give him a beating. Eddie was a block away, on a stoop, eating a sandwich. He heard his brother scream. He ran to the alley, grabbed a garbage can lid, and sent two boys to the hospital.

After that, Joe didn't talk to him for months. He was ashamed. Joe was the oldest, the firstborn, but it was Eddie who did the fighting.

"Can we go again, Eddie? *Please?*"

Thirty-four minutes to live. Eddie lifted the lap bar, gave each boy a sucking candy, retrieved his cane, then limped to the maintenance shop to cool down from the summer heat. Had he known his death was imminent, he might have gone somewhere else. Instead, he did what we all do. He went about his dull routine as if all the days in the world were still to come.

One of the shop workers, a lanky, bony-cheeked young man named Dominguez, was by the solvent sink, wiping grease off a wheel.

"Yo, Eddie," he said.

"Dom," Eddie said.

The shop smelled like sawdust. It was dark and cramped with a low ceiling and pegboard walls that held drills and saws and hammers. Skeleton parts of fun park rides were everywhere: compressors, engines, belts, lightbulbs, the top of a pirate's head. Stacked against one wall were coffee cans of nails and screws, and stacked against another wall were endless tubs of grease.

Greasing a track, Eddie would say, required no more brains than washing a dish; the only difference was you got dirtier as you did it, not cleaner. And that was the sort of work that Eddie did: spread grease, adjusted brakes, tightened bolts, checked electrical panels. Many times he had longed to leave this place, find different work, build another kind of life. But the war came. His plans never worked out. In time, he found himself graying and wearing looser pants and in a state of weary acceptance, that this was who he was and who he would always be, a man with sand in his shoes in a world of mechanical laughter and grilled frankfurters. Like his father before him, like the patch on

4 **stoop** set of steps or small porch at the entrance of a house – 14 **imminent** close, about to happen – 17 **lanky** thin and tall

his shirt, Eddie was maintenance—the head of maintenance—or as the kids sometimes called him, "the ride man at Ruby Pier."

Thirty minutes left.

"Hey, happy birthday, I hear," Dominguez said.

Eddie grunted.

"No party or nothing?"

Eddie looked at him as if he were crazy. For a moment he thought how strange it was to be growing old in a place that smelled of cotton candy.

"Well, remember, Eddie, I'm off next week, starting Monday. Going to Mexico."

Eddie nodded, and Dominguez did a little dance.

"Me and Theresa. Gonna see the whole family. Par-r-r-ty."

He stopped dancing when he noticed Eddie staring.

"You ever been?" Dominguez said.

"Been?"

"To Mexico?"

Eddie exhaled through his nose. "Kid, I never been anywhere I wasn't shipped to with a rifle."

He watched Dominguez return to the sink. He thought for a moment. Then he took a small wad of bills from his pocket and removed the only twenties he had, two of them. He held them out.

"Get your wife something nice," Eddie said.

Dominguez regarded the money, broke into a huge smile, and said, "C'mon, man. You sure?"

Eddie pushed the money into Dominguez's palm. Then he walked out back to the storage area. A small "fishing hole" had been cut into the boardwalk planks years ago, and Eddie lifted the plastic cap. He tugged on a nylon line that dropped 80 feet to the sea. A piece of bologna was still attached.

"We catch anything?" Dominguez yelled. "Tell me we caught something!"

Eddie wondered how the guy could be so optimistic. There was never anything on that line.

"One day," Dominguez yelled, "we're gonna get a halibut!"

10 **cotton candy** a sweet made by spinning sugar that has been boiled at a high temperature – 21 **to ship sb or sth somewhere:** to transport somewhere by ship

"Yep," Eddie mumbled, although he knew you could never pull a fish that big through a hole that small.

Twenty-six minutes to live. Eddie crossed the boardwalk to the south end. Business was slow. The girl behind the taffy counter was leaning on her elbows, popping her gum.

Once, Ruby Pier was *the* place to go in the summer. It had elephants and fireworks and marathon dance contests. But people didn't go to ocean piers much anymore; they went to theme parks where you paid $75 a ticket and had your photo taken with a giant furry character.

Eddie limped past the bumper cars and fixed his eyes on a group of teenagers leaning over the railing. *Great,* he told himself. *Just what I need.*

"Off," Eddie said, tapping the railing with his cane. "C'mon. It's not safe."

The teens glared at him. The car poles sizzled with electricity, *zzzap zzzap* sounds.

"It's not safe," Eddie repeated.

The teens looked at each other. One kid, who wore a streak of orange in his hair, sneered at Eddie, then stepped onto the middle rail.

"Come on, dudes, hit me!" he yelled, waving at the young drivers. "Hit m—"

Eddie whacked the railing so hard with his cane he almost snapped it in two. "MOVE IT!"

The teens ran away.

Another story went around about Eddie. As a soldier, he had engaged in combat numerous times. He'd been brave. Even won a medal. But toward the end of his service, he got into a fight with one of his own men. That's how Eddie was wounded. No one knew what happened to the other guy.

No one asked.

With 19 minutes left on earth, Eddie sat for the last time, in an old aluminum beach chair. His short, muscled arms folded like a seal's flippers across his chest. His legs were red from the sun, and his left knee still showed scars. In truth, much of Eddie's

10 **furry** ['fɜ:ri:] hairy – 11 **to limp** to walk unevenly due to an injured leg or foot – 16 **to glare at sb** to stare angrily at sb – 20 **to sneer at sb** to smile contemptuously – 35 **seal** *Seehund*

body suggested a survived encounter. His fingers were bent at awkward angles, thanks to numerous fractures from assorted machinery. His nose had been broken several times in what he called "saloon fights." His broadly jawed face might have been good-looking once, the way a prizefighter might have looked before he took too many punches.

Now Eddie just looked tired. This was his regular spot on the Ruby Pier boardwalk, behind the Jackrabbit ride, which in the 1980s was the Thunderbolt, which in the 1970s was the Steel Eel, which in the 1960s was the Lollipop Swings, which in the 1950s was Laff In The Dark, and which before that was the Stardust Band Shell.

Which was where Eddie met Marguerite.

Every life has one true-love snapshot. For Eddie, it came on a warm September night after a thunderstorm, when the boardwalk was spongy with water. She wore a yellow cotton dress, with a pink barrette in her hair. Eddie didn't say much. He was so nervous he felt as if his tongue were glued to his teeth. They danced to the music of a big band, Long Legs Delaney and his Everglades Orchestra. He bought her a lemon fizz. She said she had to go before her parents got angry. But as she walked away, she turned and waved.

That was the snapshot. For the rest of his life, whenever he thought of Marguerite, Eddie would see that moment, her waving over her shoulder, her dark hair falling over one eye, and he would feel the same arterial burst of love.

That night he came home and woke his older brother. He told him he'd met the girl he was going to marry.

"Go to sleep, Eddie," his brother groaned.

Whrrrssssh. A wave broke on the beach. Eddie coughed up something he did not want to see. He spat it away.

Whrrsssssssh. He used to think a lot about Marguerite. Not so much now. She was like a wound beneath an old bandage, and he had grown more used to the bandage.

Whrrsssssssh.

What was shingles?

Whrrrssssssh.

Sixteen minutes to live.

2 **fracture** breaking of a bone – 17 **barrette** [bə'ret] a pin for holding hair in place – 20 **fizz** a sparkling drink

No story sits by itself. Sometimes stories meet at corners and sometimes they cover one another completely, like stones beneath a river.

The end of Eddie's story was touched by another seemingly innocent story, months earlier—a cloudy night when a young man arrived at Ruby Pier with three of his friends.

The young man, whose name was Nicky, had just begun driving and was still not comfortable carrying a key chain. So he removed the single car key and put it in his jacket pocket, then tied the jacket around his waist.

For the next few hours, he and his friends rode all the fastest rides: the Flying Falcon, the Splashdown, Freddy's Free Fall, the Ghoster Coaster.

"Hands in the air!" one of them yelled.

They threw their hands in the air.

Later, when it was dark, they returned to the car lot, exhausted and laughing, drinking beer from brown paper bags. Nicky reached into his jacket pocket. He fished around. He cursed.

The key was gone.

Fourteen minutes until his death. Eddie wiped his brow with a handkerchief. Out on the ocean, diamonds of sunlight danced on the water, and Eddie stared at their nimble movement. He had not been right on his feet since the war.

But back at the Stardust Band Shell with Marguerite—there Eddie had still been graceful. He closed his eyes and allowed himself to summon the song that brought them together, the one Judy Garland sang in that movie. It mixed in his head now with the cacophony of the crashing waves and children screaming on the rides.

"You made me love you—"

Whssssshhhh.

"—do it, I didn't want to do i—"

Splllllaaaaashhhhhhh.

"—me love you—"

Eeeeeeee!

"—time you knew it, and all the—"

Chhhhewisshhhh.

"—knew it..."

16 **car lot** *(AE)* car park – 18 **to curse** to swear, use bad language – 22 **nimble** moving quickly and lightly – 26 **to summon** to recall to memory – 28 **cacophony** *BE:* [kə'kɒfəni:]; *AE:* [kæ'kɑ:fəni:] loud, chaotic noise

Eddie felt her hands on his shoulders. He squeezed his eyes tightly, to bring the memory closer.

Twelve minutes to live.

"'Scuse me."

A young girl, maybe eight years old, stood before him, blocking his sunlight. She had blonde curls and wore flip-flops and denim cutoff shorts and a lime green T-shirt with a cartoon duck on the front. Amy, he thought her name was. Amy or Annie. She'd been here a lot this summer, although Eddie never saw a mother or father.

" 'Scuuuse me," she said again. "Eddie Maint'nance?"

Eddie sighed. "Just Eddie," he said.

"Eddie?"

"Um hmm?"

"Can you make me..."

She put her hands together as if praying.

"C'mon, kiddo. I don't have all day."

"Can you make me an animal? *Can you?*"

Eddie looked up, as if he had to think about it. Then he reached into his shirt pocket and pulled out three yellow pipe cleaners, which he carried for just this purpose.

"Yesssss!" the little girl said, slapping her hands.

Eddie began twisting the pipe cleaners.

"Where's your parents?"

"Riding the rides."

"Without you?"

The girl shrugged. "My mom's with her boyfriend."

Eddie looked up. Oh.

He bent the pipe cleaners into several small loops, then twisted the loops around one another. His hands shook now, so it took longer than it used to, but soon the pipe cleaners resembled a head, ears, body, and tail.

"A rabbit?" the little girl said.

Eddie winked.

"Thaaaank you!"

She spun away, lost in that place where kids don't even know their feet are moving. Eddie wiped his brow again, then closed

4 **'Scuse me** Excuse me *(AE) (Entschuldigen Sie!)* – 20 **pipe cleaner** *Pfeifenreiniger* – 27 **to shrug** to raise one's shoulders to indicate resignation or indifference – 29 **loop** anything with a round or oval shape – 36 **to spin** to turn round fast

his eyes, slumped into the beach chair, and tried to get the old song back into his head.

A seagull squawked as it flew overhead.

How do people choose their final words? Do they realize their gravity? Are they fated to be wise?

By his 83rd birthday, Eddie had lost nearly everyone he'd cared about. Some had died young, and some had been given a chance to grow old before a disease or an accident took them away. At their funerals, Eddie listened as mourners recalled their final conversations. "*It's as if he knew he was going to die....*" some would say.

Eddie never believed that. As far as he could tell, when your time came, it came, and that was that. You might say something smart on your way out, but you might just as easily say something stupid.

For the record, Eddie's final words would be "Get back!"

Here are the sounds of Eddie's last minutes on earth. Waves crashing. The distant thump of rock music. The whirring engine of a small biplane, dragging an ad from its tail. And this.

"OH MY GOD! LOOK!"

Eddie felt his eyes dart beneath his lids. Over the years, he had come to know every noise at Ruby Pier and could sleep through them all like a lullaby.

This voice was not in the lullaby.

"OH MY GOD! LOOK!"

Eddie bolted upright. A woman with fat, dimpled arms was holding a shopping bag and pointing and screaming. A small crowd gathered around her, their eyes to the skies.

Eddie saw it immediately. Atop Freddy's Free Fall, the new "tower drop" attraction, one of the carts was tilted at an angle, as if trying to dump its cargo. Four passengers, two men, two women, held only by a safety bar, were grabbing frantically at anything they could.

1 **to slump** to let yourself fall – 5 **gravity** importance – 9 **mourner** *BE:* ['mɔːnə]; *AE:* ['mɔːrnər] people who are sad at the loss of a person they loved, esp at a funeral – 19 **biplane** an old airplane with two wings one above the other – 19 **to drag** to pull – 21 **to dart** to move quickly – 23 **lullaby** ['lʌləbaɪ] a song that is sung to children at night to make them go to sleep – 26 **to bolt** to move with great haste – 30 **cart** an open wagon as used in roller coasters or other amusement rides – 30 **to tilt** to move sideways or bend – **tilted** leaning to one side

"OH MY GOD!" the fat woman yelled. "THOSE PEOPLE! THEY'RE GONNA FALL!"

A voice squawked from the radio on Eddie's belt. "*Eddie! Eddie!*"

He pressed the button. "I see it! Get security!"

People ran up from the beach, pointing as if they had practiced this drill. *Look! Up in the sky! An amusement ride turned evil!* Eddie grabbed his cane and clomped to the safety fence around the platform base, his wad of keys jangling against his hip. His heart was racing.

Freddy's Free Fall was supposed to drop two carts in a stomach-churning descent, only to be halted at the last instant by a gush of hydraulic air. How did one cart come loose like that? It was tilted just a few feet below the upper platform, as if it had started downward then changed its mind.

Eddie reached the gate and had to catch his breath. Dominguez came running and nearly banged into him.

"Listen to me!" Eddie said, grabbing Dominguez by the shoulders. His grip was so tight, Dominguez made a pained face. "Listen to me! Who's up there?"

"Willie."

"OK. He must've hit the emergency stop. That's why the cart is hanging. Get up the ladder and tell Willie to manually release the safety restraint so those people can get out. OK? It's on the back of the cart, so you're gonna have to hold him while he leans out there. OK? Then... then, the two of ya's—the two of ya's now, not one, you got it?—the two of ya's get them out! One holds the other! Got it!?... *Got it?*"

Dominguez nodded quickly.

"Then send that damn cart down so we can figure out what happened!"

Eddie's head was pounding. Although his park had been free of any major accidents, he knew the horror stories of his business. Once, in Brighton, a bolt unfastened on a gondola ride and two people fell to their death. Another time, in Wonderland Park, a man had tried to walk across a roller coaster track; he fell through and got stuck beneath his armpits. He was wedged in, screaming, and the cars came racing toward him and... well, that was the worst.

23 **to release** to unblock – 24 **safety restraint** *Sicherheitsbügel* – 32 **to pound** to hit hard; here: to pulsate rapidly with pain – 34 **bolt** a certain type of strong screw – 37 **to wedge** to squeeze into a tiny space, to stick

Eddie pushed that from his mind. There were people all around him now, hands over their mouths, watching Dominguez climb the ladder. Eddie tried to remember the insides of Freddy's Free Fall. *Engine. Cylinders. Hydraulics. Seals. Cables.* How does a cart come loose? He followed the ride visually, from the four frightened people at the top, down the towering shaft, and into the base. *Engine. Cylinders. Hydraulics. Seals. Cables...* .

Dominguez reached the upper platform. He did as Eddie told him, holding Willie as Willie leaned toward the back of the cart to release the restraint. One of the female riders lunged for Willie and nearly pulled him off the platform. The crowd gasped.

"Wait..." Eddie said to himself.

Willie tried again. This time he popped the safety release.

"Cable..." Eddie mumbled.

The bar lifted and the crowd went "Ahhhhh." The riders were quickly pulled to the platform.

"The cable is *unraveling....*"

And Eddie was right. Inside the base of Freddy's Free Fall, hidden from view, the cable that lifted Cart No. 2 had, for the last few months, been scraping across a locked pulley. Because it was locked, the pulley had gradually ripped the cable's steel wires—as if husking an ear of corn—until they were nearly severed. No one noticed. How could they notice? Only someone who had crawled inside the mechanism would have seen the unlikely cause of the problem.

The pulley was wedged by a small object that must have fallen through the opening at a most precise moment.

A car key.

"DON'T RELEASE THE CART!" Eddie yelled. He waved his arms. "HEY! HEEEEY! IT'S THE CABLE! DON'T RELEASE THE CART! IT'LL SNAP!"

The crowd drowned him out. It cheered wildly as Willie and Dominguez unloaded the final rider. All four were safe. They hugged atop the platform.

"DOM! WILLIE!" Eddie yelled. Someone banged against his waist, knocking his walkie-talkie to the ground. Eddie bent to get it. Willie went to the controls. He put his finger on the green button. Eddie looked up.

4 **seal** *Dichtung* – 6 **shaft** *Säule, Schacht* – 11 **to gasp** to draw in breath quickly, open-mouthed – 17 **to unravel** to become undone because the fibres are separating – 20 **locked** blocked – 20 **pulley** *Flaschenzug, hier: Umlenk- oder Umleitrolle* – 23 **to sever** *BE:* ['sevə]; *AE:* ['sevər] to separate

"NO, NO, NO, DON'T!"

Eddie turned to the crowd. "GET BACK!"

Something in Eddie's voice must have caught the people's attention; they stopped cheering and began to scatter. An opening cleared around the bottom of Freddy's Free Fall.

And Eddie saw the last face of his life.

She was sprawled upon the ride's metal base, as if someone had knocked her into it, her nose running, tears filling her eyes, the little girl with the pipe-cleaner animal. Amy? Annie?

"Ma... Mom... Mom..." she heaved, almost rhythmically, her body frozen in the paralysis of crying children.

"Ma... Mom... Ma... Mom..."

Eddie's eyes shot from her to the carts. Did he have time? Her to the carts—

Whump. Too late. The carts were dropping—*Jesus, he released the brake!*—and for Eddie, everything slipped into watery motion. He dropped his cane and pushed off his bad leg and felt a shot of pain that almost knocked him down. A big step. Another step. Inside the shaft of Freddy's Free Fall, the cable snapped its final thread and ripped across the hydraulic line. Cart No. 2 was in a dead drop now, nothing to stop it, a boulder off a cliff.

In those final moments, Eddie seemed to hear the whole world: distant screaming, waves, music, a rush of wind, a low, loud, ugly sound that he realized was his own voice blasting through his chest. The little girl raised her arms. Eddie lunged. His bad leg buckled. He half flew, half stumbled toward her, landing on the metal platform, which ripped through his shirt and split open his skin, just beneath the patch that read EDDIE and MAINTENANCE. He felt two hands in his own, two small hands.

A stunning impact.

A blinding flash of light.

And then, nothing.

4 **to scatter** to go away in all directions – 7 **to sprawl** *BE:* [sprɔ:l]; *AE:* [sprɑ:l] to sit or lie with arms and legs spread out – 10 **to heave** [hi:v] to breathe in noisily and heavily – 21 **boulder** a large and heavy stone – 26 **to lunge** [lʌndʒ] to jump forwards – 27 **to buckle** to collapse – 32 **to stun** to shock or to make dizzy as happens after a blow on the head

Today Is Eddie's Birthday

It is the 1920s, a crowded hospital in one of the poorest sections of the city. Eddie's father smokes cigarettes in the waiting room, where the other fathers are also smoking cigarettes. The nurse enters with a clipboard. She calls his name. She mispronounces it. The other men blow smoke. Well?

He raises his hand.

"Congratulations," the nurse says.

He follows her down the hallway to the newborns' nursery. His shoes clap on the floor.

"Wait here," she says.

Through the glass, he sees her check the numbers of the wooden cribs. She moves past one, not his, another, not his, another, not his, another, not his.

She stops. There. Beneath the blanket. A tiny head covered in a blue cap. She checks her clipboard again, then points.

The father breathes heavily, nods his head. For a moment, his face seems to crumble, like a bridge collapsing into a river. Then he smiles.

His.

12 **crib** baby's bed

The Journey

Eddie saw nothing of his final moment on earth, nothing of the pier or the crowd or the shattered fiberglass cart.

In the stories about life after death, the soul often floats above the good-bye moment, hovering over police cars at highway accidents, or clinging like a spider to hospital-room ceilings. These are people who receive a second chance, who somehow, for some reason, resume their place in the world.

Eddie, it appeared, was not getting a second chance.

Where... ?

Where... ?

Where... ?

The sky was a misty pumpkin shade, then a deep turquoise, then a bright lime. Eddie was floating, and his arms were still extended.

Where... ?

The tower cart was falling. He remembered that. The little girl—Amy? Annie?—she was crying. He remembered that. He remembered lunging. He remembered hitting the platform. He felt her two small hands in his.

Then what?

Did I save her?

Eddie could only picture it at a distance, as if it happened years ago. Stranger still, he could not *feel* any emotions that went with it. He could only feel calm, like a child in the cradle of its mother's arms.

Where... ?

The sky around him changed again, to grapefruit yellow, then a forest green, then a pink that Eddie momentarily associated with, of all things, cotton candy.

Did I save her?

Did she live?

Where...

. . . is my worry?

Where is my pain?

That was what was missing. Every hurt he'd ever suffered, every ache he'd ever endured—it was all as gone as an expired breath. He could not feel agony. He could not feel sadness. His consciousness felt smoky, wisplike, incapable of anything but

24 **cradle** *Wiege* – 37 **agony** ['ægəni] intense feeling of suffering or pain

calm. Below him now, the colors changed again. Something was swirling. Water. An ocean. He was floating over a vast yellow sea. Now it turned melon. Now it was sapphire. Now he began to drop, hurtling toward the surface. It was faster than anything he'd ever imagined, yet there wasn't as much as a breeze on his face, and he felt no fear. He saw the sands of a golden shore.

Then he was under water.

Then everything was silent.

Where is my worry?

Where is my pain?

Today Is Eddie's Birthday

He is five years old. It is a Sunday afternoon at Ruby Pier. Picnic tables are set along the boardwalk, which overlooks the long white beach. There is a vanilla cake with blue wax candles. There is a bowl of orange juice. The pier workers are milling about, the barkers, the sideshow acts, the animal trainers, some men from the fishery. Eddie's father, as usual, is in a card game. Eddie plays at his feet. His older brother, Joe, is doing push-ups in front of a group of elderly women, who feign interest and clap politely.

Eddie is wearing his birthday gift, a red cowboy hat and a toy holster. He gets up and runs from one group to the next, pulling out the toy gun and going, "Bang, bang!"

"C'mere boy," Mickey Shea beckons from a bench.

"Bang, bang," goes Eddie.

Mickey Shea works with Eddie's dad, fixing the rides. He is fat and wears suspenders and is always singing Irish songs. To Eddie, he smells funny, like cough medicine.

"C'mere. Lemme do your birthday bumps," he says. "Like we do in Ireland."

Suddenly, Mickey's large hands are under Eddie's armpits and he is hoisted up, then flipped over and dangled by the feet. Eddie's hat falls off.

"Careful, Mickey!" Eddie's mother yells. Eddie's father looks up, smirks, then returns to his card game.

4 **to hurtle** to move rapidly – 14 **to mill about** to move around aimlessly, without order – 18 **to feign** [feɪn] **interest** to pretend to be interested – 34 **to smirk** *BE:* [smɜ:k]; *AE:* [smɜ:rk] a forced smile expressing contempt rather than pleasure

"Ho, ho. I got 'im," Mickey says. "Now. One birthday bump for every year."

Mickey lowers Eddie gently, until his head brushes the floor.

"One!"

Mickey lifts Eddie back up. The others join in, laughing. They yell, "Two! ... Three!"

Upside down, Eddie is not sure who is who. His head is getting heavy.

"Four! ..." they shout. "Five!"

Eddie is flipped right-side up and put down. Everybody claps. Eddie reaches for his hat, then stumbles over. He gets up, wobbles to Mickey Shea, and punches him in the arm.

"Ho-ho! What was that for, little man?" Mickey says. Everyone laughs. Eddie turns and runs away, three steps, before being swept into his mother's arms.

"Are you all right, my darling birthday boy?" She is only inches from his face. He sees her deep red lipstick and her plump, soft cheeks and the wave of her auburn hair.

"I was upside down," he tells her.

"I saw," she says.

She puts his hat back on his head. Later, she will walk him along the pier, perhaps take him on an elephant ride, or watch the fishermen pull in their evening nets, the fish flipping like shiny, wet coins. She will hold his hand and tell him God is proud of him for being a good boy on his birthday, and that will make the world feel right-side up again.

The Arrival

Eddie awoke in a teacup.

It was a part of some old amusement park ride—a large teacup, made of dark, polished wood, with a cushioned seat and a steel-hinged door. Eddie's arms and legs dangled over the edges. The sky continued to change colors, from a shoe-leather brown to a deep scarlet.

His instinct was to reach for his cane. He had kept it by his bed the last few years, because there were mornings when he no longer had the strength to get up without it. This embarrassed

11 **to wobble** to walk unsteadily – 18 **auburn** *BE:* ['ɔ:bən]; *AE:* ['ɑ:bərn] reddish brown – 30 **steel-hinged** [hɪndʒd] attached with joints of steel

Eddie, who used to punch men in the shoulders when he greeted them.

But now there was no cane, so Eddie exhaled and tried to pull himself up. Surprisingly, his back did not hurt. His leg did not throb. He yanked harder and hoisted himself easily over the edge of the teacup, landing awkwardly on the ground, where he was struck by three quick thoughts.

First, he felt wonderful.

Second, he was all alone.

Third, he was still on Ruby Pier.

But it was a different Ruby Pier now. There were canvas tents and vacant grassy sections and so few obstructions you could see the mossy breakwater out in the ocean. The colors of the attractions were firehouse reds and creamy whites—no teals or maroons—and each ride had its own wooden ticket booth. The teacup he had awoken in was part of a primitive attraction called Spin-O-Rama. Its sign was plywood, as were the other low-slung signs, hinged on storefronts that lined the promenade:

El Tiempo Cigars! Now, That's a Smoke!
Chowder, 10 cents!
Ride the Whipper—The Sensation of the Age!

Eddie blinked hard. This was the Ruby Pier of his childhood, some 75 years ago, only everything was new, freshly scrubbed. Over there was the Loop-the-Loop ride—which had been torn down decades ago—and over there the bathhouses and the saltwater swimming pools that had been razed in the 1950s. Over there, jutting into the sky, was the original Ferris wheel—in its pristine white paint—and beyond that, the streets of his old neighborhood and the rooftops of the crowded brick tenements, with laundry lines hanging from the windows.

Eddie tried to yell, but his voice was raspy air. He mouthed a "Hey!" but nothing came from his throat.

He grabbed at his arms and legs. Aside from his lack of voice, he felt incredible. He walked in a circle. He jumped. No pain. In the last ten years, he had forgotten what it was like to walk

5 **to throb** to pulsate with pain – 5 **to yank** to pull – 14 **teal** a bluish shade of green – 15 **ticket booth** a kiosk for selling tickets – 17 **plywood** ['plaiwʊd] wood made up of several layers of thin wood *(Schichtholz)* – 28 **pristine** completely clean and free from dirt or spots – 29 **tenement** a run-down apartment house, often occupied by poor families

without wincing or to sit without struggling to find comfort for his lower back. On the outside, he looked the same as he had that morning: a squat, barrel-chested old man in a cap and shorts and a brown maintenance jersey. But he was *limber*. So limber, in fact, he could touch behind his ankles, and raise a leg to his belly. He explored his body like an infant, fascinated by the new mechanics, a rubber man doing a rubber man stretch.

Then he ran.

Ha-ha! Running! Eddie had not truly run in more than 60 years, not since the war, but he was running now, starting with a few gingerly steps, then accelerating into a full gait, faster, faster, like the running boy of his youth. He ran along the boardwalk, past a bait-and-tackle stand for fishermen (five cents) and a bathing suit rental stand for swimmers (three cents). He ran past a chute ride called The Dipsy Doodle. He ran along the Ruby Pier Promenade, beneath magnificent buildings of Moorish design, with spires and minarets and onion-shaped domes. He ran past the Parisian Carousel, with its carved wooden horses, glass mirrors, and Wurlitzer organ, all shiny and new. Only an hour ago, it seemed, he had been scraping rust from its pieces in his shop.

He ran down the heart of the old midway, where the weight guessers, fortune-tellers, and dancing gypsies had once worked. He lowered his chin and held his arms out like a glider, and every few steps he would jump, the way children do, hoping running will turn to flying. It might have seemed ridiculous to anyone watching, this white-haired maintenance worker, all alone, making like an airplane. But the running boy is inside every man, no matter how old he gets.

And then Eddie stopped running. He heard something. A voice, tinny, as if coming through a megaphone.

"How about him, ladies and gentlemen? Have you ever seen such a horrible sight? ..."

Eddie was standing by an empty ticket kiosk in front of a large theater. The sign above read

The World's Most Curious Citizens.
Ruby Pier's Sideshow!
Holy Smoke! They're Fat! They're Skinny!

1 **to wince** [wɪnts] to tighten the muscles in your face when you feel pain – 4 **jersey** T-shirt – 4 **limber** capable of bending and flexing freely – 24 **glider** a plane that can fly without a motor, floating in the air

See the Wild Man!

The sideshow. The freak house. The ballyhoo hall. Eddie recalled them shutting this down at least 50 years ago, about the time television became popular and people didn't need sideshows to tickle their imagination.

"Look well upon this savage, born into a most peculiar handicap..."

Eddie peered into the entrance. He had encountered some odd people here. There was Jolly Jane, who weighed over 500 pounds and needed two men to push her up the stairs. There were conjoined twin sisters, who shared a spine and played musical instruments. There were men who swallowed swords, women with beards, and a pair of Indian brothers whose skin went rubbery from being stretched and soaked in oils, until it hung in bunches from their limbs.

Eddie, as a child, had felt sorry for the sideshow cast. They were forced to sit in booths or on stages, sometimes behind bars, as patrons walked past them, leering and pointing. A barker would ballyhoo the oddity, and it was a barker's voice that Eddie heard now.

"Only a terrible twist of fate could leave a man in such a pitiful condition! From the farthest corner of the world, we have brought him for your examination... ."

Eddie entered the darkened hall. The voice grew louder.

"This tragic soul has endured a perversion of nature... ."

It was coming from the other side of a stage.

"Only here, at the World's Most Curious Citizens, can you draw this near... ."

Eddie pulled aside the curtain.

"Feast your eyes upon the most unus—"

The barker's voice vanished. And Eddie stepped back in disbelief.

There, sitting in a chair, alone on the stage, was a middle-aged man with narrow, stooped shoulders, naked from the waist up. His belly sagged over his belt. His hair was closely cropped. His lips were thin and his face was long and drawn. Eddie would have long since forgotten him, were it not for one distinctive feature.

His skin was blue.

"Hello, Edward," he said. "I have been waiting for you."

2 **ballyhoo** noisy and sensational advertising

The First Person Eddie Meets in Heaven

"Don't be afraid... ." the Blue Man said, rising slowly from his chair. "Don't be afraid... ."

His voice was soothing, but Eddie could only stare. He had barely known this man. Why was he seeing him now? He was like one of those faces that pops into your dreams and the next morning you say, "You'll never guess who I dreamed about last night."

"Your body feels like a child's, right?"

Eddie nodded.

"You were a child when you knew me, that's why. You start with the same feelings you had."

Start what? Eddie thought.

The Blue Man lifted his chin. His skin was a grotesque shade, a graying blueberry. His fingers were wrinkled. He walked outside. Eddie followed. The pier was empty. The beach was empty. Was the entire planet empty?

"Tell me something," the Blue Man said. He pointed to a two-humped wooden roller coaster in the distance. The Whipper. It was built in the 1920s, before under-friction wheels, meaning the cars couldn't turn very quickly—unless you wanted them launching off the track. "The Whipper. Is it still the 'fastest ride on earth'?"

Eddie looked at the old clanking thing, which had been torn down years ago. He shook his head no.

"Ah," the Blue Man said. "I imagined as much. Things don't change here. And there's none of that peering down from the clouds, I'm afraid."

Here? Eddie thought.

The Blue Man smiled as if he'd heard the question. He touched Eddie's shoulder and Eddie felt a surge of warmth unlike anything he had ever felt before. His thoughts came spilling out like sentences.

How did I die?

"An accident," the Blue Man said.

How long have I been dead?

"A minute. An hour. A thousand years."

Where am I?

3 **to soothe** to comfort – 23 **clanking** the noise made when two pieces of metal hit each other – 26 **to peer** to look interestedly, searchingly

The Blue Man pursed his lips, then repeated the question thoughtfully. "Where are you?" He turned and raised his arms. All at once, the rides at the old Ruby Pier cranked to life: The Ferris wheel spun, the Dodgem Cars smacked into each other, the Whipper clacked uphill, and the Parisian Carousel horses bobbed on their brass poles to the cheery music of the Wurlitzer organ. The ocean was in front of them. The sky was the color of lemons.

"Where do you think?" the Blue Man asked. "Heaven."

No! Eddie shook his head violently. *NO!* The Blue Man seemed amused.

"No? It can't be heaven?" he said. "Why? Because this is where you grew up?"

Eddie mouthed the word *Yes.*

"Ah." The Blue Man nodded. "Well. People often belittle the place where they were born. But heaven can be found in the most unlikely corners. And heaven itself has many steps. This, for me, is the second. And for you, the first."

He led Eddie through the park, passing cigar shops and sausage stands and the "flat joints," where suckers lost their nickels and dimes.

Heaven? Eddie thought. Ridiculous. He had spent most of his adult life trying to get *away* from Ruby Pier. It was an amusement park, that's all, a place to scream and get wet and trade your dollars for kewpie dolls. The thought that this was some kind of blessed resting place was beyond his imagination.

He tried again to speak, and this time he heard a small grunt from his chest. The Blue Man turned.

"Your voice will come. We all go through the same thing. You cannot talk when you first arrive."

He smiled. "It helps you listen."

"There are five people you meet in heaven," the Blue Man suddenly said. "Each of us was in your life for a reason. You may not have known the reason at the time, and that is what heaven is for. For understanding your life on earth."

Eddie looked confused.

1 **to purse** *BE:* [pɜːs]; *AE:* [pɜːrs] **one's lips** *(die Lippen spitzen)* – 20 **sucker** a naive person who is easy to take advantage of

"People think of heaven as a paradise garden, a place where they can float on clouds and laze in rivers and mountains. But scenery without solace is meaningless.

"This is the greatest gift God can give you: to understand what happened in your life. To have it explained. It is the peace you have been searching for."

Eddie coughed, trying to bring up his voice. He was tired of being silent.

"I am your first person, Edward. When I died, my life was illuminated by five others, and then I came here to wait for you, to stand in your line, to tell you my story, which becomes part of yours. There will be others for you, too. Some you knew, maybe some you didn't. But they all crossed your path before they died. And they altered it forever."

Eddie pushed a sound up from his chest, as hard as he could.

"What..." he finally croaked.

His voice seemed to be breaking through a shell, like a baby chick.

"What... killed..."

The Blue Man waited patiently.

"What... killed... you?"

The Blue Man looked a bit surprised. He smiled at Eddie.

"You did," he said.

Today Is Eddie's Birthday

He is seven years old and his gift is a new baseball. He squeezes it in each hand, feeling a surge of power that runs up his arms. He imagines he is one of his heroes on the Cracker Jack collector cards, maybe the great pitcher Walter Johnson.

"Here, toss it," his brother, Joe, says.

They are running along the midway, past the game booth where, if you knock over three green bottles, you win a coconut and a straw.

"Come on, Eddie," Joe says. "Share."

Eddie stops, and imagines himself in a stadium. He throws the ball. His brother pulls in his elbows and ducks.

3 **solace** *BE:* ['sɒləs]; *AE:* ['sɑːləs] comfort or consolation – 14 **to alter** to change – 35 **to duck** to move out of the way in a downward direction (so that you are not hit by sth) *(sich ducken, in Deckung gehen)*

"Too hard!" Joe yells.

"My ball!" Eddie screams. "Dang you, Joe."

Eddie watches it thump down the boardwalk and bang off a post into a small clearing behind the sideshow tents. He runs after it. Joe follows. They drop to the ground.

"You see it?" Eddie says.

"Nuh-uh."

A whumping *noise interrupts them. A tent flap opens. Eddie and Joe look up. There is a grossly fat woman and a shirtless man with reddish hair covering his entire body. Freaks from the freak show.*

The children freeze.

"What are you wiseacres doin' back here?" the hairy man says, grinning. "Lookin' for trouble?"

Joe's lip trembles. He starts to cry. He jumps up and runs away, his arms pumping wildly. Eddie rises, too, then sees his ball against a sawhorse. He eyes the shirtless man and moves slowly toward it.

"This is mine," he mumbles. He scoops up the ball and runs after his brother.

"LISTEN, MISTER," EDDIE RASPED, "I never killed you, OK? I don't even *know* you."

The Blue Man sat on a bench. He smiled as if trying to put a guest at ease. Eddie remained standing, a defensive posture.

"Let me begin with my real name," the Blue Man said. "I was christened Joseph Corvelzchik, the son of a tailor in a small Polish village. We came to America in 1894. I was only a boy. My mother held me over the railing of the ship and this became my earliest childhood memory, my mother swinging me in the breezes of a new world.

"Like most immigrants, we had no money. We slept on a mattress in my uncle's kitchen. My father was forced to take a job in a sweatshop, sewing buttons on coats. When I was ten, he took me from school and I joined him."

Eddie watched the Blue Man's pitted face, his thin lips, his sagging chest. *Why is he telling* me *this?* Eddie thought.

4 **clearing** an empty space between houses or tents – 24 **posture** attitude, pose – 26 **to christen** ['krɪsən] to baptise and give a Christian name to sb – 33 **sweatshop** a factory, usually in the textile industry, where workers are deprived of rights and poorly paid

"I was a nervous child by nature, and the noise in the shop only made things worse. I was too young to be there, amongst all those men, swearing and complaining.

"Whenever the foreman came near, my father told me, 'Look down. Don't make him notice you.' Once, however, I stumbled and dropped a sack of buttons, which spilled over the floor. The foreman screamed that I was worthless, a worthless child, that I must go. I can still see that moment, my father pleading with him like a street beggar, the foreman sneering, wiping his nose with the back of his hand. I felt my stomach twist in pain. Then I felt something wet on my leg. I looked down. The foreman pointed at my soiled pants and laughed, and the other workers laughed, too.

"After that, my father refused to speak to me. He felt I had shamed him, and I suppose, in his world, I had. But fathers can ruin their sons, and I was, in a fashion, ruined after that. I was a nervous child, and when I grew, I was a nervous young man. Worst of all, at night, I still wet the bed. In the mornings I would sneak the soiled sheets to the washbasin and soak them. One morning, I looked up to see my father. He saw the dirty sheets, then glared at me with eyes that I will never forget, as if he wished he could snap the cord of life between us."

The Blue Man paused. His skin, which seemed to be soaked in blue fluid, folded in small fatty layers around his belt. Eddie couldn't help staring.

"I was not always a freak, Edward," he said. "But back then, medicine was rather primitive. I went to a chemist, seeking something for my nerves. He gave me a bottle of silver nitrate and told me to mix it with water and take it every night. Silver nitrate. It was later considered poison. But it was all I had, and when it failed to work, I could only assume I was not ingesting enough. So I took more. I swallowed two gulps and sometimes three, with no water.

"Soon, people were looking at me strangely. My skin was turning the color of ash.

"I was ashamed and agitated. I swallowed even more silver nitrate, until my skin went from gray to blue, a side effect of the poison."

The Blue Man paused. His voice dropped. "The factory dismissed me. The foreman said I scared the other workers. Without work, how would I eat? Where would I live?

"I found a saloon, a dark place where I could hide beneath a hat and coat. One night, a group of carnival men were in the back. They smoked cigars. They laughed. One of them, a rather small fellow with a wooden leg, kept looking at me. Finally, he approached.

"By the end of the night, I had agreed to join their carnival. And my life as a commodity had begun."

Eddie noticed the resigned look on the Blue Man's face. He had often wondered where the sideshow cast came from. He assumed there was a sad story behind every one of them.

"The carnivals gave me my names, Edward. Sometimes I was the Blue Man of the North Pole, or the Blue Man of Algeria, or the Blue Man of New Zealand. I had never been to any of these places, of course, but it was pleasant to be considered exotic, if only on a painted sign. The 'show' was simple. I would sit on the stage, half undressed, as people walked past and the barker told them how pathetic I was. For this, I was able to put a few coins in my pocket. The manager once called me the 'best freak' in his stable, and, sad as it sounds, I took pride in that. When you are an outcast, even a tossed stone can be cherished.

"One winter, I came to this pier. Ruby Pier. They were starting a sideshow called The Curious Citizens. I liked the idea of being in one place, escaping the bumpy horse carts of carnival life.

"This became my home. I lived in a room above a sausage shop. I played cards at night with the other sideshow workers, with the tinsmiths, sometimes even with your father. In the early mornings, if I wore long shirts and draped my head in a towel, I could walk along this beach without scaring people. It may not sound like much, but for me, it was a freedom I had rarely known."

He stopped. He looked at Eddie.

"Do you understand? Why we're here? This is not *your* heaven. It's mine."

Take one story, viewed from two different angles.

Take a rainy Sunday morning in July, in the late 1920s, when Eddie and his friends are tossing a baseball Eddie got for his birthday nearly a year ago. Take a moment when that ball flies over Eddie's head and out into the street. Eddie, wearing tawny pants and a wool cap, chases after it, and runs in front of an automobile, a Ford Model A. The car screeches, veers, and just misses him. He shivers, exhales, gets the ball, and races back

5 **commodity** an article that is offered for sale – 15 **pathetic** miserable, pitiful – 18 **to toss** *(inf)* to throw – 18 **to cherish** to hold dear, to treasure

to his friends. The game soon ends and the children run to the arcade to play the Erie Digger machine, with its claw-like mechanism that picks up small toys.

Now take that same story from a different angle. A man is behind the wheel of a Ford Model A, which he has borrowed from a friend to practice his driving. The road is wet from the morning rain. Suddenly, a baseball bounces across the street, and a boy comes racing after it. The driver slams on the brakes and yanks the wheel. The car skids, the tires screech.

The man somehow regains control, and the Model A rolls on. The child has disappeared in the rearview mirror, but the man's body is still affected, thinking of how close he came to tragedy. The jolt of adrenaline has forced his heart to pump furiously and this heart is not a strong one and the pumping leaves him drained. The man feels dizzy and his head drops momentarily. His automobile nearly collides with another. The second driver honks, the man veers again, spinning the wheel, pushing on the brake pedal. He skids along an avenue then turns down an alley. His vehicle rolls until it collides with the rear of a parked truck. There is a small crashing noise. The headlights shatter. The impact smacks the man into the steering wheel. His forehead bleeds. He steps from the Model A, sees the damage, then collapses onto the wet pavement. His arm throbs. His chest hurts. It is Sunday morning. The alley is empty. He remains there, unnoticed, slumped against the side of the car. The blood from his coronary arteries no longer flows to his heart. An hour passes. A policeman finds him. A medical examiner pronounces him dead. The cause of death is listed as "heart attack." There are no known relatives.

Take one story, viewed from two different angles. It is the same day, the same moment, but one angle ends happily, at an arcade, with the little boy in tawny pants dropping pennies into the Erie Digger machine, and the other ends badly, in a city morgue, where one worker calls another worker over to marvel at the blue skin of the newest arrival.

"You see?" the Blue Man whispered, having finished the story from his point of view. "Little boy?"

Eddie felt a shiver.

"Oh no," he whispered.

15 **drained** exhausted, empty – 17 **to honk** *(AE)* to use the horn of a car *(hupen)* – 20 **to shatter** to break into many little pieces – 25 **coronary arteries** blood vessels that surround the heart – 33 **morgue** *BE:* [mɔːg]; *AE:* [mɔːrg] place where dead bodies are kept before they are buried or cremated *(Leichenschauhaus)* – 37 **shiver** shaking, trembling sensation

Today Is Eddie's Birthday

He is eight years old. He sits on the edge of a plaid couch, his arms crossed in anger. His mother is at his feet, tying his shoes. His father is at the mirror, fixing his tie.

"I don't WANT to go," Eddie says.

"I know," his mother says, not looking up, "but we have to. Sometimes you have to do things when sad things happen."

"But it's my BIRTHDAY."

Eddie looks mournfully across the room at the erector set in the corner, a pile of toy metal girders and three small rubber wheels. Eddie had been making a truck. He is good at putting things together. He had hoped to show it to his friends at a birthday party. Instead, they have to go someplace and get dressed up. It isn't fair, he thinks.

His brother, Joe, dressed in wool pants and a bow tie, enters with a baseball glove on his left hand. He slaps it hard. He makes a face at Eddie.

"Those were my old *shoes," Joe says. "My new ones are better."*

Eddie winces. He hates having to wear Joe's old things.

"Stop wiggling," his mother says.

"They HURT," Eddie whines.

"Enough!" his father yells. He glares at Eddie. Eddie goes silent.

At the cemetery, Eddie barely recognizes the pier people. The men who normally wear gold lamé and red turbans are now in black suits, like his father. The women seem to be wearing the same black dress; some cover their faces in veils.

Eddie watches a man shovel dirt into a hole. The man says something about ashes. Eddie holds his mother's hand and squints at the sun. He is supposed to be sad, he knows, but he is secretly counting numbers, starting from 1, hoping that by the time he reaches 1000 he will have his birthday back.

8 **erector set** a toy with which children build models of things – 9 **girder** a long thick piece of metal, usually steel

The First Lesson

"Please; Mister," Eddie pleaded... . "I didn't know. Believe me... God help me, I didn't know."

The Blue Man nodded. "You couldn't know. You were too young."

Eddie stepped back. He squared his body as if bracing for a fight.

"But now I gotta pay," he said.

"To pay?"

"For my sin. That's why I'm here, right? Justice?"

The Blue Man smiled. "No, Edward. You are here so I can teach you something. All the people you meet here have one thing to teach you."

Eddie was skeptical. His fists stayed clenched.

"What?" he said.

"That there are no random acts. That we are all connected. That you can no more separate one life from another than you can separate a breeze from the wind."

Eddie shook his head. "We were throwing a *ball*. It was *my* stupidity, running out there like that. Why should *you* have to die on account of *me*? It ain't *fair*."

The Blue Man held out his hand. "Fairness," he said, "does not govern life and death. If it did, no good person would ever die young."

He rolled his palm upward and suddenly they were standing in a cemetery behind a small group of mourners. A priest by the gravesite was reading from a Bible. Eddie could not see faces, only the backs of hats and dresses and suit coats.

"My funeral," the Blue Man said. "Look at the mourners. Some did not even know me well, yet they came. Why? Did you ever wonder? Why people gather when others die? Why people feel they *should*?

"It is because the human spirit knows, deep down, that all lives intersect. That death doesn't just take someone, it misses someone else, and in the small distance between being taken and being missed, lives are changed.

"You say you should have died instead of me. But during my time on earth, people died instead of me, too. It happens

5 **to brace** to prepare for an attack – 13 **to clench one's fist** to close one's hand firmly – 15 **random** done or chosen without method or thinking – 20 **it ain't** *(sl)* it isn't – 26 **gravesite** the hole in the ground into which the coffin is lowered – 33 **to intersect** to cross, to be related

every day. When lightning strikes a minute after you are gone, or an airplane crashes that you might have been on. When your colleague falls ill and you do not. We think such things are random. But there is a balance to it all. One withers, another grows. Birth and death are part of a whole.

"It is why we are drawn to babies... ." He turned to the mourners. "And to funerals."

Eddie looked again at the gravesite gathering. He wondered if he'd had a funeral. He wondered if anyone came. He saw the priest reading from the Bible and the mourners lowering their heads. This was the day the Blue Man had been buried, all those years ago. Eddie had been there, a little boy, fidgeting through the ceremony, with no idea of the role he'd played in it.

"I still don't understand," Eddie whispered. "What good came from your death?"

"You lived," the Blue Man answered.

"But we barely knew each other. I might as well have been a stranger."

The Blue Man put his arms on Eddie's shoulders. Eddie felt that warm, melting sensation.

"Strangers," the Blue Man said, "are just family you have yet to come to know."

With that, the Blue Man pulled Eddie close. Instantly, Eddie felt everything the Blue Man had felt in his life rushing into him, swimming in his body, the loneliness, the shame, the nervousness, the heart attack. It slid into Eddie like a drawer being closed.

"I am leaving," the Blue Man whispered in his ear. "This step of heaven is over for me. But there are others for you to meet."

"Wait," Eddie said, pulling back. "Just tell me one thing. Did I save the little girl? At the pier. Did I save her?"

The Blue Man did not answer. Eddie slumped. "Then my death was a waste, just like my life."

"No life is a waste," the Blue Man said. "The only time we waste is the time we spend thinking we are alone."

He stepped back toward the gravesite and smiled. And as he did, his skin turned the loveliest shade of caramel—smooth and

4 **to wither** to become weaker – 8 **gathering** small crowd – 32 **to slump** to let your shoulders and head hang low with disappointment or fatigue

unblemished. It was, Eddie thought, the most perfect skin he had ever seen.

"Wait!" Eddie yelled, but he was suddenly whisked into the air, away from the cemetery, soaring above the great gray ocean. Below him, he saw the rooftops of old Ruby Pier, the spires and turrets, the flags flapping in the breeze.

Then it was gone.

SUNDAY, 3 P.M.

Back at the pier, the crowd stood silently around the wreckage of Freddy's Free Fall. Old women touched their throats. Mothers pulled their children away. Several burly men in tank tops slid to the front, as if this were something they should handle, but once they got there, they, too, only looked on, helpless. The sun baked down, sharpening the shadows, causing them to shield their eyes as if they were saluting.

How bad is it? people whispered. From the back of the crowd, Dominguez burst through, his face red, his maintenance shirt drenched in sweat. He saw the carnage.

"Ahh no, no, Eddie," he moaned, grabbing his head. Security workers arrived. They pushed people back. But then, they, too, fell into impotent postures, hands on their hips, waiting for the ambulances. It was as if all of them—the mothers, the fathers, the kids with their giant gulp soda cups—were too stunned to look and too stunned to leave. Death was at their feet, as a carnival tune played over the park speakers.

How bad is it? Sirens sounded. Men in uniforms arrived. Yellow tape was stretched around the area. The arcade booths pulled down their grates. The rides were closed indefinitely. Word spread across the beach of the bad thing that had happened, and by sunset, Ruby Pier was empty.

1 **unblemished** spotless, faultless – 17 **carnage** *BE:* ['kɑːnɪdʒ]; *AE:* ['kɑːrnɪdʒ] the violent death of people – 27 **grate** a metal frame used to protect sth (here: a shop window)

Today Is Eddie's Birthday

From his bedroom, even with the door closed, Eddie can smell the beefsteak his mother is grilling with green peppers and sweet red onions, a strong, woody odor that he loves.

"Eddd-deee!" she yells from the kitchen. "Where are you? Everyone's here!"

He rolls off the bed and puts away the comic book. He is 17 today, too old for such things, but he still enjoys the idea—colorful heroes like the Phantom, fighting the bad guys, saving the world. He has given his collection to his school-aged cousins from Romania, who came to America a few months earlier. Eddie's family met them at the docks and they moved into the bedroom that Eddie shared with his brother, Joe. The cousins cannot speak English, but they like comic books. Anyhow, it gives Eddie an excuse to keep them around.

"There's the birthday boy," his mother crows when he rambles into the room. He wears a button-down white shirt and a blue tie, which pinches his muscular neck. A grunt of hellos and raised beer glasses come from the assembled visitors, family, friends, pier workers. Eddie's father is playing cards in the corner, in a small cloud of cigar smoke.

"Hey, Ma, guess what?" Joe yells out. "Eddie met a girl last night."

"Oooh. Did he?"

Eddie feels a rush of blood.

"Yeah. Said he's gonna marry her."

"Shut yer trap," Eddie says to Joe.

Joe ignores him. "Yep, he came into the room all google-eyed, and he said, 'Joe, I met the girl I'm gonna marry!'"

Eddie seethes. "I said shut it!"

"What's her name, Eddie?" someone asks.

"Does she go to church?"

Eddie goes to his brother and socks him in the arm.

"Owww!"

"Eddie!"

"I told you to shut it!"

Joe blurts out, "And he danced with her at the Stard—!"

Whack.

15 **to crow** to make happy sounds, to say sth happily – 29 **to seethe** [si:ð] to be very angry – 32 **to sock** *(inf)* to hit hard

"Oww!"

"SHUT UP!"

"Eddie! Stop that!!"

Even the Romanian cousins look up now—fighting they understand—as the two brothers grab each other and flail away, clearing the couch, until Eddie's father puts down his cigar and yells, "Knock it off, before I slap both of ya's."

The brothers separate, panting and glaring. Some older relatives smile. One of the aunts whispers, "He must really like this girl."

Later, after the special steak has been eaten and the candles have been blown out and most of the guests have gone home, Eddie's mother turns on the radio. There is news about the war in Europe, and Eddie's father says something about lumber and copper wire being hard to get if things get worse. That will make maintenance of the park nearly impossible.

"Such awful news," Eddie's mother says. "Not at a birthday."

She turns the dial until the small box offers music, an orchestra playing a swing melody, and she smiles and hums along. Then she comes over to Eddie, who is slouched in his chair, picking at the last pieces of cake. She removes her apron, folds it over a chair, and lifts Eddie by the hands.

"Show me how you danced with your new friend," she says.

"Aw, Ma."

"Come on."

Eddie stands as if being led to his execution. His brother smirks. But his mother, with her pretty, round face, keeps humming and stepping back and forth, until Eddie falls into a dance step with her.

"Daaa daa deeee," *she sings with the melody,* ". . . when you're with meeee... da da... the stars, and the moon... the da... da... da... in June..."

They move around the living room until Eddie breaks down and laughs. He is already taller than his mother by a good six inches, yet she twirls him with ease.

"So," she whispers, "you like this girl?"

Eddie loses a step.

"It's all right," she says. "I'm happy for you."

They spin to the table, and Eddie's mother grabs Joe and pulls him up.

5 **to flail** to beat hard, to struggle – 14 **lumber** *(AE)* wood for building *(BE:* timber) – 15 **copper wire** *Kupferdraht*

"Now you two dance," she says.
"With him?"
"Ma!"

But she insists and they relent, and soon Joe and Eddie are laughing and stumbling into each other. They join hands and move, swooping up and down in exaggerated circles. Around and around the table they go, to their mother's delight, as the clarinets lead the radio melody and the Romanian cousins clap along and the final wisps of grilled steak evaporate into the party air.

The Second Person Eddie Meets in Heaven

Eddie felt his feet touch ground. The sky was changing again, from cobalt blue to charcoal gray, and Eddie was surrounded now by fallen trees and blackened rubble. He grabbed his arms, shoulders, thighs, and calves. He felt stronger than before, but when he tried to touch his toes, he could no longer do so. The limberness was gone. No more childish rubbery sensation. Every muscle he had was as tight as piano wire.

He looked around at the lifeless terrain. On a nearby hill lay a busted wagon and the rotting bones of an animal. Eddie felt a hot wind whip across his face. The sky exploded to a flaming yellow.

And once again, Eddie ran.

He ran differently now, in the hard measured steps of a soldier. He heard thunder—or something like thunder, explosions, or bomb blasts—and he instinctively fell to the ground, landed on his stomach, and pulled himself along by his forearms. The sky burst open and gushed rain, a thick, brownish downpour. Eddie lowered his head and crawled along in the mud, spitting away the dirty water that gathered around his lips.

Finally he felt his head brush against something solid. He looked up to see a rifle dug into the ground, with a helmet sitting atop it and a set of dog tags hanging from the grip. Blinking through the rain, he fingered the dog tags, then scrambled backward wildly into a porous wall of stringy vines that hung

13 **rubble** bits of broken stone, esp from a destroyed building – 19 **busted** *(AE, inf)* broken – 32 **dog tag** military identification label made of metal, worn on a chain around the neck – 34 **vine** hanging plants *(Schling- oder Kletterpflanzen)*

from a massive banyan tree. He dove into their darkness. He pulled his knees into a crouch. He tried to catch his breath. Fear had found him, even in heaven.

The name on the dog tags was his.

Young men go to war. Sometimes because they have to, sometimes because they want to. Always, they feel they are supposed to. This comes from the sad, layered stories of life, which over the centuries have seen courage confused with picking up arms, and cowardice confused with laying them down.

When his country entered the war, Eddie woke up early one rainy morning, shaved, combed back his hair, and enlisted. Others were fighting. He would, too.

His mother did not want him to go. His father, when informed of the news, lit a cigarette and blew the smoke out slowly.

"When?" was all he asked.

Since he'd never fired an actual rifle, Eddie began to practice at the shooting arcade at Ruby Pier. You paid a nickel and the machine hummed and you squeezed the trigger and fired metal slugs at pictures of jungle animals, a lion or a giraffe. Eddie went every evening, after running the brake levers at the Li'l Folks Miniature Railway. Ruby Pier had added a number of new, smaller attractions, because roller coasters, after the Depression, had become too expensive. The Miniature Railway was pretty much just that, the train cars no higher than a grown man's thigh.

Eddie, before enlisting, had been working to save money to study engineering. That was his goal—he wanted to build things, even if his brother, Joe, kept saying, "C'mon, Eddie, you aren't smart enough for that."

But once the war started, pier business dropped. Most of Eddie's customers now were women alone with children, their fathers gone to fight. Sometimes the children asked Eddie to lift them over his head, and when Eddie complied, he saw the mothers' sad smiles: He guessed it was the right lift but the wrong pair of arms. Soon, Eddie figured, he would join those distant men, and his life of greasing tracks and running brake levers would be over. War was his call to manhood. Maybe someone would miss him, too.

34 **to comply** to agree

On one of those final nights, Eddie was bent over the small arcade rifle, firing with deep concentration. *Pang! Pang!* He tried to imagine actually shooting at the enemy. *Pang!* Would they make a noise when he shot them—*pang!*—or would they just go down, like the lions and giraffes?

Pang! Pang!

"Practicing to kill, are ya, lad?"

Mickey Shea was standing behind Eddie. His hair was the color of French vanilla ice cream, wet with sweat, and his face was red from whatever he'd been drinking. Eddie shrugged and returned to his shooting. *Pang!* Another hit. *Pang!* Another.

"Hmmph," Mickey grunted.

Eddie wished Mickey would go away and let him work on his aim. He could feel the old drunk behind him. He could hear his labored breathing, the nasal hissing in and out, like a bike tire being inflated by a pump.

Eddie kept shooting. Suddenly, he felt a painful grip on his shoulder.

"Listen to me, lad." Mickey's voice was a low growl. "War is no game. If there's a shot to be made, you make it, you hear? No guilt. No hesitation. You fire and you fire and you don't think about who you're shootin' or killin' or why, y'hear me? You want to come home again, you just fire, you don't think."

He squeezed even harder.

"It's the thinking that gets you killed."

Eddie turned and stared at Mickey. Mickey slapped him hard on the cheek and Eddie instinctively raised his fist to retaliate. But Mickey belched and wobbled backward. Then he looked at Eddie as if he were going to cry. The mechanical gun stopped humming. Eddie's nickel was up.

Young men go to war, sometimes because they have to, sometimes because they want to. A few days later, Eddie packed a duffel bag and left the pier behind.

The rain stopped. Eddie, shivering and wet beneath the banyan tree, exhaled a long, hard breath. He pulled the vines apart and saw the rifle and helmet still stuck in the ground. He remembered why soldiers did this: It marked the graves of their dead.

He crawled out on his knees. Off in the distance, below a small ridge, were the remains of a village, bombed and burnt into

15 **labored** here: heavy – 27 **to retaliate** [rɪ'tælieɪt] to hit back – 30 **Eddie's nickel was up.** The money had run out, his time was over. – 39 **ridge** a long narrow range of hills

little more than rubble. For a moment, Eddie stared, his mouth slightly open, his eyes bringing the scene into tighter focus. Then his chest tightened like a man who'd just had bad news broken. This place. He knew it. It had haunted his dreams.

"Smallpox," a voice suddenly said.

Eddie spun.

"Smallpox. Typhoid. Tetanus. Yellow fever."

It came from above, somewhere in the tree.

"I never did find out what yellow fever was. Hell. I never met anyone who had it."

The voice was strong, with a slight Southern drawl and gravelly edges, like a man who'd been yelling for hours.

"I got all those shots for all those diseases and I died here anyhow, healthy as a horse."

The tree shook. Some small fruit fell in front of Eddie.

"How you like *them* apples?" the voice said.

Eddie stood up and cleared his throat.

"Come out," he said.

"Come up," the voice said.

And Eddie was in the tree, near the top, which was as tall as an office building. His legs straddled a large limb and the earth below seemed a long drop away. Through the smaller branches and thick fig leaves, Eddie could make out the shadowy figure of a man in army fatigues, sitting back against the tree trunk. His face was covered with a coal black substance. His eyes glowed red like tiny bulbs.

Eddie swallowed hard.

"Captain?" he whispered. "Is that you?"

They had served together in the army. The Captain was Eddie's commanding officer. They fought in the Philippines and they parted in the Philippines and Eddie had never seen him again. He had heard he'd died in combat.

A wisp of cigarette smoke appeared.

"They explained the rules to you, soldier?"

Eddie looked down. He saw the earth far below, yet he knew he could not fall.

"I'm dead," he said.

"You got that much right."

7 **smallpox, typhoid, tetanus, yellow fever** tropical diseases – 11 **southern drawl** American English accent spoken in the southern states of the USA – 13 **shot** injection to immunise against disease – 16 **How you like them apples?** *(sl)* How do you like these apples? – 24 **fatigues** [fə'tiːgz] military uniform

"And *you're* dead."

"Got that right, too."

"And you're... my second person?"

The Captain held up his cigarette. He smiled as if to say, *"Can you believe you get to smoke up here?"* Then he took a long drag and blew out a small white cloud.

"Betcha didn't expect me, huh?"

Eddie learned many things during the war. He learned to ride atop a tank. He learned to shave with cold water in his helmet. He learned to be careful when shooting from a foxhole, lest he hit a tree and wound himself with deflected shrapnel.

He learned to smoke. He learned to march. He learned to cross a rope bridge while carrying, all at once, an overcoat, a radio, a carbine, a gas mask, a tripod for a machine gun, a backpack, and several bandoliers on his shoulder. He learned how to drink the worst coffee he'd ever tasted.

He learned a few words in a few foreign languages. He learned to spit a great distance. He learned the nervous cheer of a soldier's first survived combat, when the men slap each other and smile as if it's over—*We can go home now!*—and he learned the sinking depression of a soldier's second combat, when he realizes the fighting does not stop at one battle, there is more and more after that.

He learned to whistle through his teeth. He learned to sleep on rocky earth. He learned that scabies are itchy little mites that burrow into your skin, especially if you've worn the same filthy clothes for a week. He learned a man's bones really do look white when they burst through the skin.

He learned to pray quickly. He learned in which pocket to keep the letters to his family and Marguerite, in case he should be found dead by his fellow soldiers. He learned that sometimes you are sitting next to a buddy in a dugout, whispering about how hungry you are, and the next instant there is a small *whoosh* and the buddy slumps over and his hunger is no longer an issue.

He learned, as one year turned to two and two years turned toward three, that even strong, muscular men vomit on their

7 **Betcha** *(sl)* I bet you – 11 **to deflect** to turn aside – 11 **shrapnel** type of ammunition – 14 **carbine** *BE:* [ˈkɑːbaɪn]; *AE:* [ˈkɑːrbiːn] automatic rifle – 15 **bandolier** *BE:* [bændˈəlɪə]; *AE:* [bændˈəlɪr] cartridge belt

shoes when the transport plane is about to unload them, and even officers talk in their sleep the night before combat.

He learned how to take a prisoner, although he never learned how to become one. Then one night, on a Philippine island, his group came under heavy fire, and they scattered for shelter and the skies were lit and Eddie heard one of his buddies, down in a ditch, weeping like a child, and he yelled at him, "Shut up, will ya!" and he realized the man was crying because there was an enemy soldier standing over him with a rifle at his head, and Eddie felt something cold at his neck and there was one behind him, too.

The Captain stubbed out his cigarette. He was older than the men in Eddie's troop, a lifetime military man with a lanky swagger and a prominent chin that gave him a resemblance to a movie actor of the day. Most of the soldiers liked him well enough, although he had a short temper and a habit of yelling inches from your face, so you could see his teeth, already yellowed from tobacco. Still, the Captain always promised he would "leave no one behind," no matter what happened, and the men took comfort in that.

"Captain..." Eddie said again, still stunned.

"Affirmative."

"Sir."

"No need for that. But much obliged."

"It's been... You look..."

"Like the last time you saw me?" He grinned, then spat over the tree branch. He saw Eddie's confused expression. "You're right. Ain't no reason to spit up here. You don't get sick, either. Your breath is always the same. And the chow is incredible."

Chow? Eddie didn't get any of this. "Captain, look. There's some mistake. I still don't know why I'm here. I had a nothing life, see? I worked maintenance. I lived in the same apartment for years. I took care of rides, Ferris wheels, roller coasters, stupid little rocket ships. It was nothing to be proud of. I just kind of drifted. What I'm saying is..."

Eddie swallowed. "What am I doing here?"

The Captain looked at him with those glowing red eyes, and Eddie resisted asking the other question he now wondered after the Blue Man: Did he kill the Captain, too?

13 **lanky** awkward – 14 **swagger** proud and stiff way of walking, usu to impress others – 28 **ain't no reason** *(sl)* there is no reason – 29 **chow** *(inf)* food

"You know, I've been wondering," the Captain said, rubbing his chin. "The men from our unit—did they stay in touch? Willingham? Morton? Smitty? Did you ever see those guys?"

Eddie remembered the names. The truth was, they had not kept in touch. War could bond men like a magnet, but like a magnet it could repel them, too. The things they saw, the things they did. Sometimes they just wanted to forget.

"To be honest, sir, we all kind of fell out." He shrugged. "Sorry."

The Captain nodded as if he'd expected as much.

"And you? You went back to that fun park where we all promised to go if we got out alive? Free rides for all GIs? Two girls per guy in the Tunnel of Love? Isn't that what you said?"

Eddie nearly smiled. That was what he'd said. What they'd all said. But when the war ended, nobody came.

"Yeah, I went back," Eddie said.

"And?"

"And... I never left. I tried. I made plans... But this damn leg. I don't know. Nothin' worked out."

Eddie shrugged. The Captain studied his face. His eyes narrowed. His voice lowered.

"You still juggle?" he asked.

"GO!... YOU GO!... YOU GO!"

The enemy soldiers screamed and poked them with bayonets. Eddie, Smitty, Morton, Rabozzo, and the Captain were herded down a steep hill, hands on their heads. Mortar shells exploded around them. Eddie saw a figure run through the trees, then fall in a clap of bullets.

He tried to take mental snapshots as they marched in the darkness—huts, roads, whatever he could make out—knowing such information would be precious for an escape. A plane roared in the distance, filling Eddie with a sudden, sickening wave of despair. It is the inner torture of every captured soldier, the short distance between freedom and seizure. If Eddie could only jump up and grab the wing of that plane, he could fly away from this mistake.

Instead, he and the others were bound at the wrists and ankles. They were dumped inside a bamboo barracks. The barracks

5 **to bond** to establish a link – 6 **to repel** to push back – 8 **to fall out** to stop having contact – 22 **to juggle** to throw, catch and keep in the air several objects at the same time – 37 **wrist** joint between hand and arm – 37 **ankle** joint between leg and foot

sat on stilts above the muddy ground, and they remained there for days, weeks, months, forced to sleep on burlap sacks stuffed with straw. A clay jug served as their toilet. At night, the enemy guards would crawl under the hut and listen to their conversations. As time passed, they said less and less.

They grew thin and weak. Their ribs grew visible—even Rabozzo, who had been a chunky kid when he enlisted. Their food consisted of rice balls filled with salt and, once a day, some brownish broth with grass floating in it. One night, Eddie plucked a dead hornet from the bowl. It was missing its wings. The others stopped eating.

Their captors seemed unsure of what to do with them. In the evenings, they would enter with bayonets and wiggle their blades at the Americans' noses, yelling in a foreign language, waiting for answers. It was never productive.

There were only four of them, near as Eddie could tell, and the Captain guessed that they, too, had drifted away from a larger unit and were, as often happens in real war, making it up day by day. Their faces were gaunt and bony, with dark nubs of hair. One looked too young to be a soldier. Another had the most crooked teeth Eddie had ever seen. The Captain called them Crazy One, Crazy Two, Crazy Three, and Crazy Four.

"We don't want to know their names," he said. "And we don't want them knowing ours."

Men adapt to captivity, some better than others. Morton, a skinny, chattering youth from Chicago, would fidget whenever he heard noises from outside, rubbing his chin and mumbling, "Oh, damn, oh damn, oh damn..." until the others told him to shut up. Smitty, a fireman's son from Brooklyn, was quiet most of the time, but he often seemed to be swallowing something, his Adam's apple loping up and down; Eddie later learned he was chewing on his tongue. Rabozzo, the young redheaded kid from Portland, Oregon, kept a poker face during the waking hours, but at night he often woke up screaming, "Not me! Not me!"

Eddie mostly seethed. He clenched a fist and slapped it into his palm, hours on end, knuckles to skin, like the anxious baseball player he had been in his youth. At night, he dreamed he was back at the pier, on the Derby Horse carousel, where five customers raced in circles until the bell rang. He was racing

37 **palm** inner part of the hand

his buddies, or his brother, or Marguerite. But then the dream turned, and the four Crazies were on the adjacent ponies, poking at him, sneering.

Years of waiting at the pier—for a ride to finish, for the waves to pull back, for his father to speak to him—had trained Eddie in the art of patience. But he wanted out, and he wanted revenge. He ground his jaws and he slapped his palm and he thought about all the fights he'd been in back in his old neighborhood, the time he'd sent two kids to the hospital with a garbage can lid. He pictured what he'd do to these guards if they didn't have guns.

Then one morning, the prisoners were awakened by screaming and flashing bayonets and the four Crazies had them up and bound and led down into a shaft. There was no light. The ground was cold. There were picks and shovels and metal buckets.

"It's a goddamn coal mine," Morton said.

From that day forward, Eddie and the others were forced to strip coal from the walls to help the enemy's war effort. Some shoveled, some scraped, some carried pieces of slate and built triangles to hold up the ceiling. There were other prisoners there, too, foreigners who didn't know English and who looked at Eddie with hollow eyes. Speaking was prohibited. One cup of water was given every few hours. The prisoners' faces, by the end of the day, were hopelessly black, and their necks and shoulders throbbed from leaning over.

For the first few months of this captivity, Eddie went to sleep with Marguerite's picture in his helmet propped up in front of him. He wasn't much for praying, but he prayed just the same, making up the words and keeping count each night, saying, "Lord, I'll give you these six days if you give me six days with her. ... I'll give you these nine days if I get nine days with her. ...I'll give you these sixteen days if I get sixteen days with her...."

Then, during the fourth month, something happened. Rabozzo developed an ugly skin rash and severe diarrhea. He couldn't eat a thing. At night, he sweated through his filthy clothes until they were soaking wet. He soiled himself. There

20 **slate** hard, flat, grey stone *(Schiefer)* – 29 **not to be much for praying** = not to be one for, i.e. he doesn't usually or often pray – 35 **rash** red spots which are sometimes itchy or painful, caused by heat; an allergic reaction or a disease

were no clean clothes to give him so he slept naked on the burlap, and the Captain placed his sack over him like a blanket.

The next day, down in the mine, Rabozzo could barely stand. The four Crazies showed no pity. When he slowed, they poked him with sticks to keep him scraping.

"Leave him be," Eddie growled.

Crazy Two, the most brutal of their captors, slammed Eddie with a bayonet butt. He went down, a shot of pain spreading between his shoulder blades. Rabozzo scraped a few more pieces of coal, then collapsed. Crazy Two screamed at him to get up.

"He's sick!" Eddie yelled, struggling to his feet.

Crazy Two slammed him down again.

"Shut up, Eddie," Morton whispered. "For your own good."

Crazy Two leaned over Rabozzo. He pulled back his eyelids. Rabozzo moaned. Crazy Two made an exaggerated smile and cooed, as if dealing with a baby. He went, "Ahh," and laughed. He laughed looking at all of them, making eye contact, making sure they were watching him. Then he pulled out his pistol, rammed it into Rabozzo's ear, and shot him in the head.

Eddie felt his body rip in half. His eyes blurred and his brain went numb. The echo of the gunshot hung in the mine as Rabozzo's face soaked into a spreading puddle of blood. Morton put his hands over his mouth. The Captain looked down. Nobody moved.

Crazy Two kicked black dirt over the body, then glared at Eddie and spat at his feet. He yelled something at Crazy Three and Crazy Four, both of whom seemed as stunned as the prisoners. For a moment, Crazy Three shook his head and mumbled, as if saying a prayer, his eyelids lowered and his lips moving furiously. But Crazy Two waved the gun and yelled again and Crazy Three and Crazy Four slowly lifted Rabozzo's body by its feet and dragged it along the mine floor, leaving a trail of wet blood, which, in the darkness, looked like spilt oil. They dropped him against a wall, next to a pickax.

After that, Eddie stopped praying. He stopped counting days. He and the Captain spoke only of escaping before they all met the same fate. The Captain figured the enemy war effort was desperate, that was why they needed every half-dead prisoner to scrape coal. Each day in the mine there were fewer and fewer bodies. At night, Eddie heard bombing; it seemed to be getting

12 **to struggle** to make a great effort

closer. If things got too bad, the Captain figured, their captors would bail out, destroy everything. He had seen ditches dug beyond the prisoner barracks and large oil barrels positioned up the steep hill.

"The oil's for burning the evidence," the Captain whispered. "They're digging our graves."

Three weeks later, under a hazy-mooned sky, Crazy Three was inside the barracks, standing guard. He had two large rocks, almost the size of bricks, which, in his boredom, he tried to juggle. He kept dropping them, picking them up, tossing them high, and dropping them again. Eddie, covered in black ash, looked up, annoyed at the thudding noise. He'd been trying to sleep. But now he lifted himself slowly. His vision cleared. He felt his nerves pricking to life.

"Captain..." he whispered. "You ready to move?"

The Captain raised his head. "What're you thinking?"

"Them rocks." Eddie nodded toward the guard.

"What about 'em?" the Captain said.

"I can juggle," Eddie whispered.

The Captain squinted. "What?"

But Eddie was already yelling at the guard, "Hey! Yo! You're doing it wrong!"

He made a circular motion with his palms. "This way! You do it this way! Gimme!"

He held out his hands. "I can juggle. Gimme."

Crazy Three looked at him cautiously. Of all the guards, Eddie felt, he had his best chance with this one. Crazy Three had occasionally sneaked the prisoners pieces of bread and tossed them through the small hut hole that served as a window. Eddie made the circular motion again and smiled. Crazy Three approached, stopped, went back for his bayonet, then walked the two rocks over to Eddie.

"Like this," Eddie said, and he began to juggle effortlessly. He had learned when he was seven years old, from an Italian sideshow man who juggled six plates at once. Eddie had spent countless hours practicing on the boardwalk—pebbles, rubber balls, whatever he could find. It was no big deal. Most pier kids could juggle.

2 **to bail out** to leave – 20 **to squint** to close one's eyes partly

But now he worked the two rocks furiously, juggling them faster, impressing the guard. Then he stopped, held the rocks out, and said, "Get me another one."

Crazy Three grunted.

"*Three* rocks, see?" Eddie held up three fingers. "*Three.*"

By now, Morton and Smitty were sitting up. The Captain was moving closer.

"Where are we going here?" Smitty mumbled.

"If I can get one more rock..." Eddie mumbled back.

Crazy Three opened the bamboo door and did what Eddie'd hoped he would do: He yelled for the others. Crazy One appeared with a fat rock and Crazy Two followed him in. Crazy Three thrust the rock at Eddie and yelled something. Then he stepped back, grinned at the others, and motioned for them to sit, as if to say, "Watch this."

Eddie tossed the rocks into a rhythmic weave. Each one was as big as his palm. He sang a carnival tune. *"Da, da-da-da daaaaa..."* The guards laughed. Eddie laughed. The Captain laughed. Forced laughter, buying time.

"Get *clo-ser,*" Eddie sang, pretending the words were part of the melody. Morton and Smitty slid gently in, feigning interest.

The guards were enjoying the diversion. Their posture slackened. Eddie tried to swallow his breathing. Just a little longer. He threw one rock high into the air, then juggled the lower two, then caught the third, then did it again.

"Ahhh," Crazy Three said, despite himself.

"You like that?" Eddie said. He was juggling faster now. He kept tossing one rock high and watching his captors' eyes as they followed it into the air. He sang, *"Da, da-da-da daaa,"* then, *"When I count to three,"* then, *"Da, da-da-da daaaa..."* then, *"Captain, the guy on the lefffft..."*

Crazy Two frowned suspiciously, but Eddie smiled the way the jugglers back at Ruby Pier smiled when they were losing the audience. "Lookie here, lookie here, lookie here!" Eddie cooed. "Greatest show on earth, buddy boy!"

Eddie went faster, then counted, "One... two..." then tossed a rock much higher than before. The Crazies watched it rise.

"Now!" Eddie yelled. In mid-juggle he grabbed a rock and, like the good baseball pitcher he had always been, whipped it hard

8 **Where are we going here?** What are we going to do next? – 23 **to slacken** to become less tense – 26 **despite oneself** without really wanting to – 32 **to frown** to wrinkle one's forehead

into the face of Crazy Two, breaking his nose. Eddie caught the second rock and threw it, left-handed, square into the chin of Crazy One, who fell back as the Captain jumped him, grabbing his bayonet. Crazy Three, momentarily frozen, reached for his pistol and fired wildly as Morton and Smitty tackled his legs. The door burst open and Crazy Four ran in, and Eddie threw the last rock at him and missed his head by inches, but as he ducked, the Captain was waiting against the wall with the bayonet, which he drove through Crazy Four's rib cage so hard the two of them tumbled through the door. Eddie, powered by adrenaline, leaped on Crazy Two and pounded his face harder than he had ever pounded anyone back on Pitkin Avenue. He grabbed a loose rock and slammed it against his skull, again and again, until he looked at his hands and saw a hideous purplish goo that he realized was blood and skin and coal ash, mixed together—then he heard a gunshot and grabbed his head, smearing the goo on his temples. He looked up and saw Smitty standing over him, holding an enemy pistol. Crazy Two's body went slack. He was bleeding from the chest.

"For Rabozzo," Smitty mumbled.

Within minutes, all four guards were dead.

The prisoners, thin and barefoot and covered in blood, were running now for the steep hill. Eddie had expected gunfire, more guards to fight, but there was no one. The other huts were empty. In fact, the entire camp was empty. Eddie wondered how long it had been just the four Crazies and them.

"The rest probably took off when they heard the bombing," the Captain whispered. "We're the last group left."

The oil barrels were pitched at the first rise of the hill. Less than 100 yards away was the entrance to the coal mine. There was a supply hut nearby and Morton made sure it was empty, then ran inside; he emerged with an armful of grenades, rifles, and two primitive-looking flamethrowers.

"Let's burn it down," he said.

Today Is Eddie's Birthday

The cake reads "Good luck! Fight hard!" and on the side, along the vanilla-frosted edge, someone has added the words, "Come

15 **goo** slime

home soon," in blue squiggly letters, but the "o-o-n" is squeezed together, so it reads more like "son" or "Come home son."

Eddie's mother has already cleaned and pressed the clothes he will wear the next day. She's hung them on a hanger on his bedroom closet doorknob and put his one pair of dress shoes beneath them.

Eddie is in the kitchen, fooling with his young Romanian cousins, his hands behind his back as they try to punch his stomach. One points out the kitchen window at the Parisian Carousel, which is lit for the evening customers.

"Horses!" the child exclaims.

The front door opens and Eddie hears a voice that makes his heart jump, even now. He wonders if this is a weakness he shouldn't be taking off to war.

"Hiya, Eddie," Marguerite says.

And there she is, in the kitchen doorway, looking wonderful, and Eddie feels that familiar tickle in his chest. She brushes a bit of rainwater from her hair and smiles. She has a small box in her hands.

"I brought you something. For your birthday, and, well... for your leaving, too."

She smiles again. Eddie wants to hug her so badly, he thinks he'll burst. He doesn't care what is in the box. He only wants to remember her holding it out for him. As always, with Marguerite, Eddie mostly wants to freeze time.

"This is swell," he says.

She laughs. "You haven't opened it yet."

"Listen." He moves closer. "Do you—"

"Eddie!" someone yells from the other room. "Come on and blow out the candles."

"Yeah! We're hungry!"

"Oh, Sal, shush!"

"Well, we are."

There is cake and beer and milk and cigars and a toast to Eddie's success, and there is a moment where his mother begins to cry and she hugs her other son, Joe, who is staying stateside on account of his flat feet.

Later that night, Eddie walks Marguerite along the promenade. He knows the names of every ticket taker and food vendor and they all wish him luck. Some of the older women get teary-eyed, and Eddie figures they have sons of their own, already gone.

26 **swell** *(AE, inf)* very good – 36 **stateside** in the USA – 39 **vendor** seller

He and Marguerite buy saltwater taffy, molasses and teaberry and root beer flavors. They pick out pieces from the small white bag, playfully fighting each other's fingers. At the penny arcade, Eddie pulls on a plaster hand and the arrow goes past "clammy" and "harmless" and "mild," all the way to "hot stuff."

"You're really strong," Marguerite says.

"Hot stuff," Eddie says, making a muscle.

At the end of the night, they stand on the boardwalk in a fashion they have seen in the movies, holding hands, leaning against the railing. Out on the sand, an old ragpicker has built a small fire from sticks and torn towels and is huddling by it, settled in for the night.

"You don't have to ask me to wait," Marguerite says suddenly.

Eddie swallows.

"I don't?"

She shakes her head. Eddie smiles. Saved from a question that has caught in his throat all night, he feels as if a string has just shot from his heart and looped around her shoulders, pulling her close, making her his. He loves her more in this moment than he thought he could ever love anyone.

A drop of rain hits Eddie's forehead. Then another. He looks up at the gathering clouds.

"Hey, Hot Stuff?" Marguerite says. She smiles but then her face droops and she blinks back water, although Eddie cannot tell if it is raindrops or tears.

"Don't get killed, OK?" she says.

A freed soldier is often furious. The days and nights he lost, the torture and humiliation he suffered—it all demands a fierce revenge, a balancing of the accounts.

So when Morton, his arms full of stolen weapons, said to the others, "Let's burn it down," there was quick if not logical agreement. Inflated by their new sense of control, the men scattered with the enemy's firepower, Smitty to the entrance of the mine shaft, Morton and Eddie to the oil barrels. The Captain went in search of a transport vehicle.

"Five minutes, then back here!" he barked. "That bombing's gonna start soon and we need to be gone. Got it? Five minutes!"

10 **ragpicker** *(AE)* sb who earns a living by picking up garbage in the streets – 28 **humiliation** [hjuːmɪliːˈeɪʃən] the feeling that one has lost one's self-respect or self-worth – 29 **revenge** action of paying back for a wrong one has suffered

Which was all it took to destroy what had been their home for nearly half a year. Smitty dropped the grenades down the mine shaft and ran. Eddie and Morton rolled two barrels into the hut complex, pried them open, then, one by one, fired the nozzles of their newly acquired flamethrowers and watched the huts ignite.

"Burn!" Morton yelled.

"Burn!" Eddie yelled.

The mine shaft exploded from below. Black smoke rose from the entrance. Smitty, his work done, ran toward the meeting point. Morton kicked his oil barrel into a hut and unleashed a rope-like burst of flame.

Eddie watched, sneered, then moved down the path to the final hut. It was larger, more like a barn, and he lifted his weapon. *This was over,* he said to himself. *Over.* All these weeks and months in the hands of those bastards, those subhuman guards with their bad teeth and bony faces and the dead hornets in their soup. He didn't know what would happen to them next, but it could not be any worse than what they had endured.

Eddie squeezed the trigger. *Whoosh*. The fire shot up quickly. The bamboo was dry, and within a minute the walls of the barn were melting in orange and yellow flames. Off in the distance, Eddie heard the rumble of an engine—the Captain, he hoped, had found something to escape in—and then, suddenly, from the skies, the first sounds of bombing, the noise they had been hearing every night. It was even closer now, and Eddie realized whoever it was would see the flames. They might be rescued. He might be going home! He turned to the burning barn and...

What was that?

He blinked.

What was that?

Something darted across the door opening. Eddie tried to focus. The heat was intense, and he shielded his eyes with his free hand. He couldn't be sure, but he thought he'd just seen a small figure running inside the fire.

"Hey!" Eddie yelled, stepping forward, lowering his weapon. "HEY!" The roof of the barn began to crumble, splashing sparks and flame. Eddie jumped back. His eyes watered. Maybe it was a shadow.

"EDDIE! NOW!"

4 **to pry** to force – 6 **to ignite** to start burning – 30 **to blink** to open and close your eyes quickly

Morton was up the path, waving for Eddie to come. Eddie's eyes were stinging. He was breathing hard. He pointed and yelled, "I think there's someone in there!"

Morton put a hand to his ear. "What?"

"Someone... in... there!"

Morton shook his head. He couldn't hear. Eddie turned and was almost certain he saw it again, there, crawling inside the burning barn, a child-size figure. It had been more than two years since Eddie had seen anything besides grown men, and the shadowy shape made him think suddenly of his small cousins back at the pier and the Li'l Folks Miniature Railway he used to run and the roller coasters and the kids on the beach and Marguerite and her picture and all that he'd shut from his mind for so many months.

"HEY! COME OUT!" he yelled, dropping the flamethrower, moving even closer. "I WON'T SHOO—"

A hand grabbed his shoulder, yanking him backward. Eddie spun, his fist clenched. It was Morton, yelling, "EDDIE! We gotta go NOW!"

Eddie shook his head. "No—no—wait—wait—wait, I think there's someone in th—"

"There's nobody in there! NOW!"

Eddie was desperate. He turned back to the barn. Morton grabbed him again. This time Eddie spun around and swung wildly, hitting him in the chest. Morton fell to his knees. Eddie's head was pounding. His face twisted in anger. He turned again to the flames, his eyes nearly shut. *There. Was that it? Rolling behind a wall? There?*

He stepped forward, convinced something innocent was being burned to death in front of him. Then the rest of the roof collapsed with a roar, casting sparks like electric dust that rained down on his head.

In that instant, the whole of the war came surging out of him like bile. He was sickened by the captivity and sickened by the murders, sickened by the blood and goo drying on his temples, sickened by the bombing and the burning and the futility of it all. At that moment he just wanted to salvage something, a piece of Rabozzo, a piece of himself, something, and he staggered into the flaming wreckage, madly convinced that there was a soul

2 **to sting** to burn with pain – 31 **roar** loud noise – 34 **bile** [baɪl] gall – 36 **futility** [fjuːˈtɪləti:] uselessness – 37 **to salvage** to save

inside every black shadow. Planes roared overhead and shots from their guns rang out in drumbeats.

Eddie moved as if in a trance. He stepped past a burning puddle of oil, and his clothes caught fire from behind. A yellow flame moved up his calf and thigh. He raised his arms and hollered.

"I'LL HELP YOU! COME OUT! I WON'T SHOO—"

A piercing pain ripped through Eddie's leg. He screamed a long, hard curse then crumbled to the ground. Blood was spewing below his knee. Plane engines roared. The skies lit in bluish flashes.

He lay there, bleeding and burning, his eyes shut against the searing heat, and for the first time in his life, he felt ready to die. Then someone yanked him backward, rolling him in the dirt, extinguishing the flames, and he was too stunned and weak to resist, he rolled like a sack of beans. Soon he was inside a transport vehicle and the others were around him, telling him to hang on, hang on. His back was burned and his knee had gone numb and he was getting dizzy and tired, so very tired.

The captain nodded slowly, as he recalled those last moments.

"You remember anything about how you got out of there?" he asked.

"Not really," Eddie said.

"It took two days. You were in and out of consciousness. You lost a lot of blood."

"We made it though," Eddie said.

"Yeaaah." The Captain drew the word out and punctuated it with a sigh. "That bullet got you pretty good."

In truth, the bullet had never been fully removed. It had cut through several nerves and tendons and shattered against a bone, fracturing it vertically. Eddie had two surgeries. Neither cured the problem. The doctors said he'd be left with a limp, one likely to get worse with age as the misshapen bones deteriorated. "The best we can do," he was told. Was it? Who could say? All Eddie knew was that he'd awoken in a medical unit and his life was never the same. His running was over. His dancing was over. Worse, for some reason, the way he used to feel about things was over, too. He withdrew. Things seemed

6 **to holler** to shout out loud – 19 **numb** [nʌm] without feeling – 30 **tendon** a cord which joins a muscle to a bone *(Sehne)* – 34 **to deteriorate** to become worse – 38 **to withdraw** to keep away from others

silly or pointless. War had crawled inside of Eddie, in his leg and in his soul. He learned many things as a soldier. He came home a different man.

"Did you know," the Captain said, "that I come from three generations of military?"

Eddie shrugged.

"Yep. I knew how to fire a pistol when I was six. In the mornings, my father would inspect my bed, actually bounce a quarter on the sheets. At the dinner table it was always, 'Yes, sir,' and, 'No, sir.'

"Before I entered the service, all I did was take orders. Next thing I knew, I was giving them.

"Peacetime was one thing. Got a lot of wise-guy recruits. But then the war started and the new men flooded in—young men, like you—and they were all saluting me, wanting me to tell them what to do. I could see the fear in their eyes. They acted as if I knew something about war that was classified. They thought I could keep them alive. You did, too, didn't you?"

Eddie had to admit he did.

The Captain reached back and rubbed his neck. "I couldn't, of course. I took my orders, too. But if I couldn't keep you alive, I thought I could at least keep you together. In the middle of a big war, you go looking for a small idea to believe in. When you find one, you hold it the way a soldier holds his crucifix when he's praying in a foxhole.

"For me, that little idea was what I told you guys every day. No one gets left behind."

Eddie nodded. "That meant a lot," he said.

The Captain looked straight at him. "I hope so," he said.

He reached inside his breast pocket, took out another cigarette, and lit up.

"Why do you say that?" Eddie asked.

The Captain blew smoke, then motioned with the end of the cigarette toward Eddie's leg.

"Because I was the one," he said, "who shot you."

Eddie looked at his leg, dangling over the tree branch. The surgery scars were back. So was the pain. He felt a welling of

8 **to bounce a quarter on the sheets** to make a coin move up and down on the sheets of a bed to see if it is properly made – 13 **wise-guy** arrogant person who makes unnecessary comments – 17 **classified** secret, confidential

something inside him that he had not felt since before he died, in truth, that he had not felt in many years: a fierce, surging flood of anger, and a desire to hurt something. His eyes narrowed and he stared at the Captain, who stared back blankly, as if he knew what was coming. He let the cigarette fall from his fingers.

"Go ahead," he whispered.

Eddie screamed and lunged with a windmill swing, and the two men fell off the tree branch and tumbled through limbs and vines, wrestling and falling all the way down.

"WHY? You bastard! You bastard! Not you! WHY?" They were grappling now on the muddy earth. Eddie straddled the Captain's chest, pummeling him with blows to the face. The Captain did not bleed. Eddie shook him by the collar and banged his skull against the mud. The Captain did not blink. Instead, he rolled from side to side with each punch, allowing Eddie his rage. Finally, with one arm, he grabbed Eddie and flipped him over.

"Because," he said calmly, his elbow across Eddie's chest, "we would have lost you in that fire. You would have died. And it wasn't your time."

Eddie panted hard. "My... time?"

The Captain continued. "You were obsessed with getting in there. You damn near knocked Morton out when he tried to stop you. We had a minute to get out and, damn your strength, you were too tough to fight."

Eddie felt a final surge of rage and grabbed the Captain by the collar. He pulled him close. He saw the teeth stained yellow by tobacco.

"My... leggggg!" Eddie seethed. "My *life*!"

"I took your leg," the Captain said, quietly, "to save your life."

Eddie let go and fell back exhausted. His arms ached. His head was spinning. For so many years, he had been haunted by that one moment, that one mistake, when his whole life changed.

"There was nobody in that hut. What was I *thinking*? If only I didn't go in there… ." His voice dropped to a whisper. "Why didn't I just *die*?"

"No one gets left behind, remember?" the Captain said. "What happened to you—I've seen it happen before. A soldier reaches a certain point and then he can't go anymore. Sometimes it's in the middle of the night. A man'll just roll out of his tent and start

12 **to pummel** to hit repeatedly, very hard and fast – 20 **to pant** to breathe with great difficulty – 22 **to knock sb out** to hit sb so hard that they lose consciousness

walking, barefoot, half naked, like he's going home, like he lives just around the corner.

"Sometimes it's in the middle of a fight. Man'll drop his gun, and his eyes go blank. He's just done. Can't fight anymore. Usually he gets shot.

"Your case, it just so happened, you snapped in front of a fire about a minute before we were done with this place. I couldn't let you burn alive. I figured a leg wound would heal. We pulled you out of there, and the others got you to a medical unit."

Eddie's breathing smacked like a hammer in his chest. His head was smeared with mud and leaves. It took him a minute to realize the last thing the Captain had said.

"The others?" Eddie said. "What do you mean, 'the *others*'?"

The Captain rose. He brushed a twig from his leg.

"Did you ever see me again?" he asked.

Eddie had not. He had been airlifted to the military hospital, and eventually, because of his handicap, was discharged and flown home to America. He had heard, months later, that the Captain had not made it, but he figured it was some later combat with some other unit. A letter arrived eventually, with a medal inside, but Eddie put it away, unopened. The months after the war were dark and brooding, and he forgot details and had no interest in collecting them. In time, he changed his address.

"It's like I told you," the Captain said. "Tetanus? Yellow fever? All those shots? Just a big waste of my time."

He nodded in a direction over Eddie's shoulder, and Eddie turned to look.

What he saw, suddenly, was no longer the barren hills but the night of their escape, the hazy moon in the sky, the planes coming in, the huts on fire. The Captain was driving the transport with Smitty, Morton, and Eddie inside. Eddie was across the backseat, burned, wounded, semiconscious, as Morton tied a tourniquet above his knee. The shelling was getting closer. The black sky lit up every few seconds, as if the sun were flickering on and off. The transport swerved as it reached the top of a hill, then stopped. There was a gate, a makeshift thing of wood and wire, but because the ground dropped off sharply on both sides, they could not go around it. The Captain grabbed a rifle and jumped

17 **to discharge** to release from military service – 22 **brooding** depressive – 32 **semi-conscious** *BE:* [semɪˈkɒnʃəs]; *AE:* [semɪˈkɑːnʃəs] only partly aware of what is going on – 32 **tourniquet** *BE:* [ˈtʊənɪkeɪ]; *AE:* ˈtʊnɪket] a bandage that stops blood flowing from a wound

out. He shot the lock and pushed the gate open. He motioned for Morton to take the wheel, then pointed to his eyes, signaling he would check the path ahead, which curled into a thicket of trees. He ran, as best he could in his bare feet, 50 yards beyond the turn in the road.

The path was clear. He waved to his men. A plane zoomed overhead and he lifted his eyes to see whose side it was. It was at that moment, while he was looking to the heavens, that a small click sounded beneath his right foot.

The land mine exploded instantly, like a burping flame from the earth's core. It blew the Captain 20 feet into the air and split him into pieces, one fiery lump of bone and gristle and a hundred chunks of charred flesh, some of which flew over the muddy earth and landed in the banyan trees.

The Second Lesson

"Aw, Jesus," Eddie said, closing his eyes, dropping his head backward. "Aw, God. Aw, God! I had no idea, sir. It's sick. It's awful!"

The Captain nodded and looked away. The hills had returned to their barren state, the animal bones and the broken cart and the smoldering remains of the village. Eddie realized this was the Captain's burial ground. No funeral. No coffin. Just his shattered skeleton and the muddy earth.

"You've been waiting here all this time?" Eddie whispered.

"Time," the Captain said, "is not what you think." He sat down next to Eddie. "Dying? Not the end of everything. We think it is. But what happens on earth is only the beginning."

Eddie looked lost.

"I figure it's like in the Bible, the Adam and Eve deal?" the Captain said. "Adam's first night on earth? When he lays down to sleep? He thinks it's all over, right? He doesn't know what sleep is. His eyes are closing and he thinks he's leaving this world, right?

"Only he isn't. He wakes up the next morning and he has a fresh new world to work with, but he has something else, too. He has his yesterday."

13 **charred** burned

The Captain grinned. "The way I see it, that's what we're getting here, soldier. That's what heaven is. You get to make sense of your yesterdays."

He took out his plastic cigarette pack and tapped it with his finger. "You followin' this? I was never all that hot at teaching."

Eddie watched the Captain closely. He had always thought of him as so much older. But now, with some of the coal ash rubbed from his face, Eddie noticed the scant lines on his skin and the full head of dark hair. He must have only been in his 30s.

"You been here since you died," Eddie said, "but that's twice as long as you lived."

The Captain nodded.

"I've been waitin' for you."

Eddie looked down.

"That's what the Blue Man said."

"Well, *he* was too. He was part of your life, part of why you lived and how you lived, part of the story you needed to know, but he told you and he's beyond here now, and in a short bit, I'm gonna be as well. So listen up. Because here's what you need to know from me."

Eddie felt his back straighten.

"Sacrifice," the captain said. "You made one. I made one. We all make them. But you were angry over yours. You kept thinking about what you lost.

"You didn't get it. Sacrifice is a part of life. It's *supposed* to be. It's not something to regret. It's something to *aspire* to. Little sacrifices. Big sacrifices. A mother works so her son can go to school. A daughter moves home to take care of her sick father.

"A man goes to war... ."

He stopped for a moment and looked off into the cloudy gray sky.

"Rabozzo didn't die for nothing, you know. He sacrificed for his country, and his family knew it, and his kid brother went on to be a good soldier and a great man because he was inspired by it.

5 **to be hot at sth** *(inf)* to be very good at sth – 8 **scant** not many, few – 23 **sacrifice** giving sth up, or doing without sth, for the good of others *(Opfer)* – 27 **to aspire to sth** to aim for sth which is good or great

"I didn't die for nothing, either. That night, we might have all driven over that land mine. Then the four of us would have been gone."

Eddie shook his head. "But you… ." He lowered his voice. "You lost your life."

The Captain smacked his tongue on his teeth. "That's the thing. Sometimes when you sacrifice something precious, you're not really losing it. You're just passing it on to someone else."

The Captain walked over to the helmet, rifle, and dog tags, the symbolic grave, still stuck in the ground. He placed the helmet and tags under one arm, then plucked the rifle from the mud and threw it like a javelin. It never landed. Just soared into the sky and disappeared. The Captain turned.

"I shot you, all right," he said, "and you lost something, but you gained something as well. You just don't know it yet. I gained something, too."

"What?"

"I got to keep my promise. I didn't leave you behind."

He held out his palm.

"Forgive me about the leg?"

Eddie thought for a moment. He thought about the bitterness after his wounding, his anger at all he had given up. Then he thought of what the Captain had given up and he felt ashamed. He offered his hand. The Captain gripped it tightly.

"That's what I've been waiting for."

Suddenly, the thick vines dropped off the banyan branches and melted with a hiss into the ground. New, healthy branches emerged in a yawning spread, covered in smooth, leathery leaves and pouches of figs. The Captain only glanced up, as if he'd been expecting it. Then, using his open palms, he wiped the remaining ash from his face.

"Captain?" Eddie said.

"Yeah?"

"Why here? You can pick anywhere to wait, right? That's what the Blue Man said. So why this place?"

The Captain smiled. "Because I died in battle. I was killed in these hills. I left the world having known almost nothing but war—war talk, war plans, a war family.

"My wish was to see what the world looked like *without* a war. Before we started killing each other."

Eddie looked around. "But this *is* war."

"To you. But our eyes are different," the Captain said. "What you see ain't what I see."

He lifted a hand and the smoldering landscape transformed. The rubble melted, trees grew and spread, the ground turned from mud to lush, green grass. The murky clouds pulled apart like curtains, revealing a sapphire sky. A light, white mist fell in above the treetops, and a peach-colored sun hung brilliantly above the horizon, reflected in the sparkling oceans that now surrounded the island. It was pure, unspoiled, untouched beauty.

Eddie looked up at his old commanding officer, whose face was clean and whose uniform was suddenly pressed.

"This," the Captain said, raising his arms, "is what I see."

He stood for a moment, taking it in.

"By the way, I don't smoke anymore. That was all in your eyes, too." He chuckled. "Why would I smoke in heaven?"

He began to walk off.

"Wait," Eddie yelled. "I gotta know something. My death. At the pier. Did I save that girl? I felt her hands, but I can't remember—"

The Captain turned and Eddie swallowed his words, embarrassed to even be asking, given the horrible way the Captain had died.

"I just want to know, that's all," he mumbled.

The Captain scratched behind his ear. He looked at Eddie sympathetically. "I can't tell you, soldier."

Eddie dropped his head.

"But someone can."

He tossed the helmet and tags. "Yours."

Eddie looked down. Inside the helmet flap was a crumpled photo of a woman that made his heart ache all over again. When he looked up, the Captain was gone.

MONDAY, 7.30 a.m.

The morning after the accident, Dominguez came to the shop early, skipping his routine of picking up a bagel and a soft drink for breakfast. The park was closed, but he came in anyhow, and he turned on the water at the sink. He ran his hands under the

5 **murky** dark and gloomy – 12 **to press** to smooth with a hot iron – 16 **to chuckle** to laugh quietly – 34 **to skip** to leave out

flow, thinking he would clean some of the ride parts. Then he shut off the water and abandoned the idea. It seemed twice as quiet as it had a minute ago.

"What's up?"

Willie was at the shop door. He wore a green tank top and baggy jeans. He held a newspaper. The headline read "Amusement Park Tragedy."

"Hard time sleeping," Dominguez said.

"Yeah." Willie slumped onto a metal stool. "Me, too."

He spun a half circle on the stool, looking blankly at the paper. "When you think they'll open us up again?"

Dominguez shrugged. "Ask the police."

They sat quietly for a while, shifting their postures as if taking turns. Dominguez sighed. Willie reached inside his shirt pocket, fishing for a stick of gum. It was Monday. It was morning. They were waiting for the old man to come in and get the workday started.

The Third Person Eddie Meets in Heaven

A sudden wind lifted Eddie, and he spun like a pocket watch on the end of a chain. An explosion of smoke engulfed him, swallowing his body in a flume of colors. The sky seemed to pull in, until he could feel it touching his skin like a gathered blanket. Then it shot away and exploded into jade. Stars appeared, millions of stars, like salt sprinkled across the greenish firmament.

Eddie blinked. He was in the mountains now, but the most remarkable mountains, a range that went on forever, with snow-capped peaks, jagged rocks, and sheer purple slopes. In a flat between two crests was a large, black lake. A moon reflected brightly in its water.

Down the ridge, Eddie noticed a flickering of colored light that changed rhythmically, every few seconds. He stepped in that direction—and realized he was ankle-deep in snow. He lifted his foot and shook it hard. The flakes fell loose, glistening with a golden sheen. When he touched them, they were neither cold nor wet.

20 **flume** tall pillar – 28 **crest** the top line of a hill

Where am I now? Eddie thought. Once again, he took stock of his body, pressing on his shoulders, his chest, his stomach. His arm muscles remained tight, but his midsection was looser, flabbier. He hesitated, then squeezed his left knee. It throbbed in pain and Eddie winced. He had hoped upon leaving the Captain that the wound would disappear. Instead, it seemed he was becoming the man he'd been on earth, scars and fat and all. Why would heaven make you relive your own decay?

He followed the flickering lights down the narrow ridge. This landscape, stark and silent, was breathtaking, more like how he'd imagined heaven. He wondered, for a moment, if he had somehow finished, if the Captain had been wrong, if there were no more people to meet. He came through the snow around a rock ledge to the large clearing from which the lights originated. He blinked again—this time in disbelief.

There, in the snowy field, sitting by itself, was a boxcar-shaped building with a stainless steel exterior and a red barrel roof. A sign above it blinked the word: *"EAT."*

A diner.

Eddie had spent many hours in places like this. They all looked the same—high-backed booths, shiny countertops, a row of small-paned windows across the front, which, from the outside, made customers appear like riders in a railroad car. Eddie could make out figures through those windows now, people talking and gesturing. He walked up the snowy steps to the double-paned door. He peered inside.

An elderly couple was sitting to his right, eating pie; they took no notice of him. Other customers sat in swivel chairs at the marble counter or inside booths with their coats on hooks. They appeared to be from different decades: Eddie saw a woman with a 1930s high-collared dress and a long-haired young man with a 1960s peace sign tattooed on his arm. Many of the patrons appeared to have been wounded. A black man in a work shirt was missing an arm. A teenage girl had a deep gash across her face. None of them looked over when Eddie rapped on the window. He saw cooks wearing white paper hats, and plates of steaming food on the counter awaiting serving—food in the most succulent colors: deep red sauces, yellow butter creams.

1 **to take stock** examine, to concentrate on – 8 **decay** process of becoming older and weaker – 10 **stark** bare – 14 **rock ledge** shelf, flat area of rock *(Felsvorsprung)* – 19 **diner** *(AE)* small, cheap restaurant that is usually open all day. Early diners resembled dining cars in trains.

His eyes moved along to the last booth in the right-hand corner. He froze.

What he saw, he could not have seen.

"No," he heard himself whisper. He turned back from the door. He drew deep breaths. His heart pounded. He spun around and looked again, then banged wildly on the windowpanes.

"No!" Eddie yelled. "No! No!" He banged until he was sure the glass would break. "No!" He kept yelling until the word he wanted, a word he hadn't spoken in decades, finally formed in his throat. He screamed that word then—he screamed it so loudly that his head throbbed. But the figure inside the booth remained hunched over, oblivious, one hand resting on the table, the other holding a cigar, never looking up, no matter how many times Eddie howled it, over and over again:

"Dad! Dad! Dad!"

Today Is Eddie's Birthday

In the dim and sterile hallway of the V.A. hospital, Eddie's mother opens the white bakery box and rearranges the candles on the cake, making them even, 12 on one side, 12 on the other. The rest of them—Eddie's father, Joe, Marguerite, Mickey Shea—stand around her, watching.

"Does anyone have a match?" she whispers.

They pat their pockets. Mickey fishes a pack from his jacket, dropping two loose cigarettes on the floor. Eddie's mother lights the candles. An elevator pings down the hall. A gurney emerges.

"All right then, let's go," she says.

The small flames wiggle as they move together. The group enters Eddie's room singing softly. "Happy birthday to you, happy birthday to—"

The soldier in the next bed wakes up yelling, "WHAT THE HELL?" He realizes where he is and drops back down, embarrassed. The song, once interrupted, seems too heavy to lift again, and only Eddie's mother's voice, shaking in its solitude, is able to continue.

12 **oblivious** not paying attention – 16 **dim** not very well lit – 24 **to ping** to make a sharp metallic sound – 24 **gurney** *(AE)* a means for transporting ill or wounded people

"Happy birthday dear Ed-die..." then quickly, "happybirthday-toyou."

Eddie props himself against a pillow. His burns are bandaged. His leg is in a long cast. There is a pair of crutches by the bed. He looks at these faces and he is consumed by a desire to run away.

Joe clears his throat. "Well, hey, you look pretty good," he says. The others quickly agree. Good. Yes. Very good.

"Your mom got a cake," Marguerite whispers.

Eddie's mother steps forward, as if it's her turn. She presents the cardboard box.

Eddie mumbles, "Thanks, Ma."

She looks around. "Now where should we put this?"

Mickey grabs a chair. Joe clears a small tabletop. Marguerite moves Eddie's crutches. Only his father does not shuffle for the sake of shuffling. He stands against the back wall, a jacket over his arm, staring at Eddie's leg, encased in plaster from thigh to ankle.

Eddie catches his eye. His father looks down and runs his hand over the windowsill. Eddie tightens every muscle in his body and attempts, by sheer will, to force the tears back into their ducts.

ALL PARENTS DAMAGE their children. It cannot be helped. Youth, like pristine glass, absorbs the prints of its handlers. Some parents smudge, others crack, a few shatter childhoods completely into jagged little pieces, beyond repair.

The damage done by Eddie's father was, at the beginning, the damage of neglect. As an infant, Eddie was rarely held by the man, and as a child, he was mostly grabbed by the arm, less with love than with annoyance. Eddie's mother handed out the tenderness; his father was there for the discipline.

On Saturdays, Eddie's father took him to the pier. Eddie would leave the apartment with visions of carousels and globs of cotton candy, but after an hour or so, his father would find a familiar face and say, "Watch the kid for me, will ya?" Until his father returned, usually late in the afternoon, often drunk, Eddie stayed in the custody of an acrobat or an animal trainer.

Still, for countless hours of his boardwalk youth, Eddie waited for his father's attention, sitting on railings or squatting in his

4 **crutch** a wooden or metal stick that fits under the armpit and is used by injured or disabled people to help them move about – 14 **to shuffle** to walk without lifting your feet; here: to move about aimlessly – 20 **duct** tube or canal – 23 **to smudge** to make dirty, to leave fingerprints – 28 **annoyance** anger

short pants atop tool chests in the repair shop. Often he'd say, "I can help, I can help!" but the only job entrusted him was crawling beneath the Ferris wheel in the morning, before the park opened, to collect the coins that had fallen from customers' pockets the night before.

At least four evenings a week, his father played cards. The table had money, bottles, cigarettes, and rules. Eddie's rule was simple: Do not disturb. Once he tried to stand next to his father and look at his cards, but the old man put down his cigar and erupted like thunder, smacking Eddie's face with the back of his hand. "Stop breathing on me," he said. Eddie burst into tears and his mother pulled him to her waist, glaring at her husband. Eddie never got that close again.

Other nights, when the cards went bad and the bottles had been emptied and his mother was already asleep, his father brought his thunder into Eddie and Joe's bedroom. He raked through the meager toys, hurling them against the wall. Then he made his sons lie facedown on the mattress while he pulled off his belt and lashed their rear ends, screaming that they were wasting his money on junk. Eddie used to pray for his mother to wake up, but even the times she did, his father warned her to "stay out of it." Seeing her in the hallway, clutching her robe, as helpless as he was, made it all even worse.

The hands on Eddie's childhood glass then were hard and calloused and red with anger, and he went through his younger years whacked, lashed, and beaten. This was the second damage done, the one after neglect. The damage of violence. It got so that Eddie could tell by the thump of the footsteps coming down the hall how hard he was going to get it.

Through it all, despite it all, Eddie privately adored his old man, because sons will adore their fathers through even the worst behavior. It is how they learn devotion. Before he can devote himself to God or a woman, a boy will devote himself to his father, even foolishly, even beyond explanation.

And on occasion, as if to feed the weakest embers of a fire, Eddie's father let a wrinkle of pride crack the veneer of his disinterest. At the baseball field by the 14th Avenue schoolyard, his father stood behind the fence, watching Eddie play. If Eddie smacked

1 **tool chest** furniture with drawers for keeping tools – 16 **he raked through the meagre toys** he angrily searched the few and cheap toys – 25 **calloused** ['kæləst] with rough skin from hard work – 26 **to whack** to hit hard – 35 **embers** hot and glowing remains of a fire

the ball to the outfield, his father nodded, and when he did, Eddie leaped around the bases. Other times, when Eddie came home from an alley fight, his father would notice his scraped knuckles or split lip. He would ask, “What happened to the other guy?” and Eddie would say he got him good. This, too, met with his father’s approval. When Eddie attacked the kids who were bothering his brother—“the hoodlums,” his mother called them—Joe was ashamed and hid in his room, but Eddie’s father said, “Never mind him. You’re the strong one. Be your brother’s keeper. Don’t let nobody touch him.”

When Eddie started junior high, he mimicked his father’s summer schedule, rising before the sun, working at the park until nightfall. At first, he ran the simpler rides, maneuvering the brake levers, bringing train cars to a gentle stop. In later years, he worked in the repair shop. Eddie’s father would test him with maintenance problems. He’d hand him a broken steering wheel and say, “Fix it.” He’d point out a tangled chain and say, “Fix it.” He’d carry over a rusty fender and some sandpaper and say, “Fix it.” And every time, upon completion of the task, Eddie would walk the item back to his father and say, “It’s fixed.”

At night they would gather at the dinner table, his mother plump and sweating, cooking by the stove, his brother, Joe, talking away, his hair and skin smelling from seawater. Joe had become a good swimmer, and his summer work was at the Ruby Pier pool. Joe talked about all the people he saw there, their swimsuits, their money. Eddie’s father was not impressed. Once Eddie overheard him talking to his mother about Joe. “That one,” he said, “ain’t tough enough for anything but water.”

Still, Eddie envied the way his brother looked in the evenings, so tanned and clean. Eddie’s fingernails, like his father’s, were stained with grease, and at the dinner table Eddie would flick them with his thumbnail, trying to get the dirt out. He caught his father watching him once and the old man grinned.

“Shows you did a hard day’s work,” he said, and he held up his own dirty fingernails, before wrapping them around a glass of beer.

By this point—already a strapping teenager—Eddie only nodded back. Unbeknownst to him, he had begun the ritual of semaphore with his father, forsaking words or physical affection.

11 **to mimic** to imitate – 38 **Unbeknownst** *BE:* [ʌnbɪˈnəʊnst]; *AE:* [ʌnbɪˈnoʊnst] **to him** without him knowing – 38 **ritual of semaphore** communicating without talking, by exchanging looks and gestures – 39 **to forsake** to leave behind, to abandon

It was all to be done internally. You were just supposed to know it, that's all. Denial of affection. The damage done.

And then, one night, the speaking stopped altogether. This was after the war, when Eddie had been released from the hospital and the cast had been removed from his leg and he had moved back into the family apartment on Beachwood Avenue. His father had been drinking at the nearby pub and he came home late to find Eddie asleep on the couch. The darkness of combat had left Eddie changed. He stayed indoors. He rarely spoke, even to Marguerite. He spent hours staring out the kitchen window, watching the carousel ride, rubbing his bad knee. His mother whispered that he "just needed time," but his father grew more agitated each day. He didn't understand depression. To him it was weakness.

"Get up," he yelled now, his words slurring, "and get a job."

Eddie stirred. His father yelled again.

"Get up... and get a job!"

The old man was wobbling, but he came toward Eddie and pushed him. "Get up and get a job! Get up and get a job! Get up... and... *GET A JOB*!"

Eddie rose to his elbows.

"Get up and get a job! Get up and—"

"ENOUGH!" Eddie yelled, surging to his feet, ignoring the burst of pain in his knee. He glared at his father, his face just inches away. He could smell the bad breath of alcohol and cigarettes.

The old man glanced at Eddie's leg. His voice lowered to a growl. "See? You... ain't... so... hurt."

He reeled back to throw a punch, but Eddie moved on instinct and grabbed his father's arm mid-swing. The old man's eyes widened. This was the first time Eddie had ever defended himself, the first time he had ever done anything besides receive a beating as if he deserved it. His father looked at his own clenched fist, short of its mark, and his nostrils flared and his teeth gritted and he staggered backward and yanked his arm free. He stared at Eddie with the eyes of a man watching a train pull away.

He never spoke to his son again.

This was the final handprint on Eddie's glass. Silence. It haunted their remaining years. His father was silent when

15 **his words slurring** talking indistinctly, not clearly

Eddie moved into his own apartment, silent when Eddie took a cab-driving job, silent at Eddie's wedding, silent when Eddie came to visit his mother. She begged and wept and beseeched her husband to change his mind, to let it go, but Eddie's father would only say to her, through a clenched jaw, what he said to others who made the same request: "That boy raised a hand to me." And that was the end of the conversation.

All parents damage their children. This was their life together. Neglect. Violence. Silence. And now, someplace beyond death, Eddie slumped against a stainless steel wall and dropped into a snowbank, stung again by the denial of a man whose love, almost inexplicably, he still coveted, a man ignoring him, even in heaven. His father. The damage done.

"Don't be angry," a woman's voice said. "He can't hear you."

Eddie jerked his head up. An old woman stood before him in the snow. Her face was gaunt, with sagging cheeks, rose-colored lipstick, and tightly pulled-back white hair, thin enough in parts to reveal the pink scalp beneath it. She wore wire-rimmed spectacles over narrow blue eyes.

Eddie could not recall her. Her clothes were before his time, a dress made of silk and chiffon, with a bib-like bodice stitched with white beads and topped with a velvet bow just below her neck. Her skirt had a rhinestone buckle and there were snaps and hooks up the side. She stood with elegant posture, holding a parasol with both hands. Eddie guessed she'd been rich.

"Not always rich," she said, grinning as if she'd heard him. "I was raised much like you were, in the back end of the city, forced to leave school when I was fourteen. I was a working girl. So were my sisters. We gave every nickel back to the family—"

Eddie interrupted. He didn't want another story. "Why can't my father hear me?" he demanded.

She smiled. "Because his spirit—safe and sound—is part of my eternity. But he is not really here. You are."

"Why does my father have to be safe for *you*?"

She paused.

"Come," she said.

Suddenly they were at the bottom of the mountain. The light from the diner was now just a speck, like a star that had fallen into a crevice.

5 **clenched** tightly closed – 12 **to covet** to long for

"Beautiful, isn't it?" the old woman said. Eddie followed her eyes. There was something about her, as if he'd seen her photograph somewhere.

"Are you... my third person?"

"I am at that," she said.

Eddie rubbed his head. *Who was this woman?* At least with the Blue Man, at least with the Captain, he had some recollection of their place in his life. Why a stranger? Why now? Eddie had once hoped death would mean a reunion with those who went before him. He had attended so many funerals, polishing his black dress shoes, finding his hat, standing in a cemetery with the same despairing question: *Why are they gone and I'm still here?* His mother. His brother. His aunts and uncles. His buddy Noel. Marguerite. "One day," the priest would say, "we will all be together in the Kingdom of Heaven."

Where were they, then, if this was heaven? Eddie studied this strange older woman. He felt more alone than ever.

"Can I see Earth?" he whispered.

She shook her head no.

"Can I talk to God?"

"You can always do that."

He hesitated before asking the next question.

"Can I go back?"

She squinted. "Back?"

"Yeah, back," Eddie said. "To my life. To that last day. Is there something I can do? Can I promise to be good? Can I promise to go to church all the time? Something?"

"Why?" She seemed amused.

"Why?" Eddie repeated. He swiped at the snow that had no cold, with the bare hand that felt no moisture. "Why? Because this place don't make no sense to me. Because I don't feel like no angel, if that's what I'm supposed to feel like. Because I don't feel like I got it all figured out. I can't even remember my own death. I can't remember the accident. All I remember are these two little hands—this little girl I was trying to save, see? I was pulling her out of the way and I must've grabbed her hands and that's when I..."

He shrugged.

"Died?" the old woman said, smiling. "Passed away? Moved on? Met your Maker?"

31 **this place don't make no sense** *(sl)* this place doesn't make any sense

"Died," he said, exhaling. "And that's all I remember. Then you, the others, all this. Ain't you supposed to have peace when you die?"

"You have peace," the old woman said, "when you make it with yourself."

"Nah," Eddie said, shaking his head. "Nah, you don't." He thought about telling her the agitation he'd felt every day since the war, the bad dreams, the inability to get excited about much of anything, the times he went to the docks alone and watched the fish pulled in by the wide rope nets, embarrassed because he saw himself in those helpless, flopping creatures, snared and beyond escape.

He didn't tell her that. Instead he said, "No offense, lady, but I don't even know you."

"But I know you," she said.

Eddie sighed.

"Oh yeah? How's that?"

"Well," she said, "if you have a moment."

She sat down then, although there was nothing to sit on. She simply rested on the air and crossed her legs, ladylike, keeping her spine straight. The long skirt folded neatly around her. A breeze blew, and Eddie caught the faint scent of perfume.

"As I mentioned, I was once a working girl. My job was serving food in a place called the Seahorse Grille. It was near the ocean where you grew up. Perhaps you remember it?"

She nodded toward the diner, and it all came back to Eddie. Of course. That place. He used to eat breakfast there. A greasy spoon, they called it. They'd torn it down years ago.

"You?" Eddie said, almost laughing. "You were a waitress at the Seahorse?"

"Indeed," she said, proudly. "I served dockworkers their coffee and longshoremen their crab cakes and bacon.

"I was an attractive girl in those years, I might add. I turned away many a proposal. My sisters would scold me. 'Who are you to be so choosy?' they would say. 'Find a man before it's too late.'

"Then one morning, the finest-looking gentleman I had ever seen walked through the door. He wore a chalk-stripe suit and a derby hat. His dark hair was neatly cut and his mustache

2 **ain't you** *(sl)* aren't you – 13 **no offense** I do not mean to offend you – 21 **spine** backbone

covered a constant smile. He nodded when I served him and I tried not to stare. But when he spoke with his colleague, I could hear his heavy, confident laughter. Twice I caught him looking in my direction. When he paid his bill, he said his name was Emile and he asked if he might call on me. And I knew, right then, my sisters would no longer have to hound me for a decision.

"Our courtship was exhilarating, for Emile was a man of means. He took me places I had never been, bought me clothes I had never imagined, paid for meals I had never experienced in my poor, sheltered life. Emile had earned his wealth quickly, from investments in lumber and steel. He was a spender, a risk taker—he went over the boards when he got an idea. I suppose that is why he was drawn to a poor girl like me. He abhorred those who were born into wealth, and rather enjoyed doing things the 'sophisticated people' would never do.

"One of those things was visiting seaside resorts. He loved the attractions, the salty food, the gypsies and fortune-tellers and weight guessers and diving girls. And we both loved the sea. One day, as we sat in the sand, the tide rolling gently to our feet, he asked for my hand in marriage.

"I was overjoyed. I told him yes and we heard the sounds of children playing in the ocean. Emile went over the boards again and swore that soon he would build a resort park just for me, to capture the happiness of this moment—to stay eternally young."

The old woman smiled. "Emile kept his promise. A few years later, he made a deal with the railroad company, which was looking for a way to increase its riders on the weekend. That's how most amusement parks were built, you know."

Eddie nodded. He knew. Most people didn't. They thought amusement parks were constructed by elves, built with candy canes. In fact, they were simply business opportunities for railroad companies, who erected them at the final stops of routes, so commuters would have a reason to ride on weekends. *You know where I work?* Eddie used to say. *The end of the line. That's where I work.*

"Emile," the old woman continued, "built the most wonderful place, a massive pier using timber and steel he already owned. Then came the magical attractions—races and rides and

13 **to abhor** to dislike very much – 15 **sophisticated** intellectual – 17 **gypsy** *(derog)* nomadic people – 24 **eternally** forever – 31 **elf** small, magical people or fairies – 34 **commuter** sb who travels regularly by train, bus or car to work

boat trips and tiny railways. There was a carousel imported from France and a Ferris wheel from one of the international exhibitions in Germany. There were towers and spires and thousands of incandescent lights, so bright that at night, you could see the park from a ship's deck on the ocean.

"Emile hired hundreds of workers, municipal workers and carnival workers and foreign workers. He brought in animals and acrobats and clowns. The entrance was the last thing finished, and it was truly grand. Everyone said so. When it was complete, he took me there with a cloth blindfold over my eyes. When he removed the blindfold, I saw it."

The old woman took a step back from Eddie. She looked at him curiously, as if she were disappointed.

"The entrance?" she said. "Don't you remember? Didn't you ever wonder about the name? Where you worked? Where your father worked?"

She touched her chest softly with her white-gloved fingers. Then she dipped, as if formally introducing herself.

"I," she said, "am Ruby."

Today Is Eddie's Birthday

He is 33. He wakes with a jolt, gasping for breath. His thick, black hair is matted with sweat. He blinks hard against the darkness, trying desperately to focus on his arm, his knuckles, anything to know that he is here, in the apartment over the bakery, and not back in the war, in the village, in the fire. That dream. Will it ever stop?

It is just before 4 a.m. No point in going back to sleep. He waits until his breathing subsides, then slowly rolls off the bed, trying not to wake his wife. He puts his right leg down first, out of habit, avoiding the inevitable stiffness of his left. Eddie begins every morning the same way. One step and one hobble.

In the bathroom, he checks his bloodshot eyes and splashes water on his face. It is always the same dream: Eddie wandering through the flames in the Philippines on his last night of war. The village huts are engulfed in fire, and there is a constant, high-pitched squealing noise. Something invisible hits Eddie's legs

18 **to dip** to bend forwards a little – 22 **knuckle** [ˈnʌkl] the joint of a finger of a closed hand – 27 **his breathing subsides** he breathes more calmly

and he swats at it but misses, and then swats again and misses again. The flames grow more intense, roaring like an engine, and then Smitty appears, yelling for Eddie, yelling, "Come on! Come on!" Eddie tries to speak but when he opens his mouth, the high-pitched squeal emerges from his throat. Then something grabs his legs, pulling him under the muddy earth.

And then he wakes up. Sweating. Panting. Always the same. The worst part is not the sleeplessness. The worst part is the general darkness the dream leaves over him, a gray film that clouds the day. Even his happy moments feel encased, like holes jabbed in a hard sheet of ice.

He dresses quietly and goes down the stairs. The taxi is parked by the corner, its usual spot, and Eddie wipes the moisture from its windshield. He never speaks about the darkness to Marguerite. She strokes his hair and says, "What's wrong?" and he says, "Nothing, I'm just beat," and leaves it at that. How can he explain such sadness when she is supposed to make him happy? The truth is he cannot explain it himself. All he knows is that something stepped in front of him, blocking his way, until in time he gave up on things, he gave up studying engineering and he gave up on the idea of traveling. He sat down in his life. And there he remained.

This night, when Eddie returns from work, he parks the taxi by the corner. He comes slowly up the stairs. From his apartment, he hears music, a familiar song.

"You made me love you
I didn't want to do it,
I didn't want to do it...."

He opens the door to see a cake on the table and a small white bag, tied with ribbon.

"Honey?" Marguerite yells from the bedroom. "Is that you?"

He lifts the white bag. Taffy. From the pier.

"Happy birthday to you..." Marguerite emerges, singing in her soft sweet voice. She looks beautiful, wearing the print dress Eddie likes, her hair and lips done up. Eddie feels the need to inhale, as if undeserving of such a moment. He fights the darkness within him, "Leave me alone," *he tells it.* "Let me feel this the way I should feel it."

Marguerite finishes the song and kisses him on the lips.

"Want to fight me for the taffy?" she whispers.

He moves to kiss her again. Someone raps on the door.

1 **to swat** *BE:* [swɒt]; *AE:* [swɑːt] to hit quickly and violently – 16 **beat** *(AE, inf)* tired

"Eddie! Are you in there? Eddie?"

Mr. Nathanson, the baker, lives in the ground-level apartment behind the store. He has a telephone. When Eddie opens the door, he is standing in the doorway, wearing a bathrobe. He looks concerned.

"Eddie," he says. "Come down. There's a phone call. I think something happened to your father."

"I am Ruby."

It suddenly made sense to Eddie, why the woman looked familiar. He had seen a photograph, somewhere in the back of the repair shop, among the old manuals and paperwork from the park's initial ownership.

"The old entrance..." Eddie said.

She nodded in satisfaction. The original Ruby Pier entrance had been something of a landmark, a giant arching structure based on a historic French temple, with fluted columns and a coved dome at the top. Just beneath that dome, under which all patrons would pass, was the painted face of a beautiful woman. This woman. Ruby.

"But that thing was destroyed a long time ago," Eddie said. "There was a big..."

He paused.

"Fire," the old woman said. "Yes. A very big fire." She dropped her chin, and her eyes looked down through her spectacles, as if she were reading from her lap.

"It was Independence Day, the Fourth of July—a holiday. Emile loved holidays. 'Good for business,' he'd say. If Independence Day went well, the entire summer might go well. So Emile arranged for fireworks. He brought in a marching band. He even hired extra workers, roustabouts mostly, just for that weekend.

"But something happened the night before the celebration. It was hot, even after the sun went down, and a few of the roustabouts chose to sleep outside, behind the work sheds. They lit a fire in a metal barrel to roast their food.

"As the night went on, there was drinking and carousing. The workers got ahold of some of the smaller fireworks. They set

15 **arching** shaped like an arch – 30 **roustabout** *(AE)* unskilled worker (*here:* workers who helped out on the pier for the weekend)

them off. The wind blew. The sparks flew. Everything in those days was made of lathe and tar...."

She shook her head. "The rest happened quickly. The fire spread to the midway and the food stalls and on to the animal cages. The roustabouts ran off. By the time someone came to our home to wake us, Ruby Pier was in flames. From our window we saw the horrible orange blaze. We heard the horses' hooves and the steamer engines of the fire companies. People were in the street.

"I begged Emile not to go, but that was fruitless. Of course he would go. He would go to the raging fire and he would try to salvage his years of work and he would lose himself in anger and fear and when the entrance caught fire, the entrance with my name and my picture, he lost all sense of where he was, too. He was trying to throw buckets of water when a column collapsed upon him."

She put her fingers together and raised them to her lips. "In the course of one night, our lives were changed forever. Risk taker that he was, Emile had acquired only minimal insurance on the pier. He lost his fortune. His splendid gift to me was gone.

"In desperation, he sold the charred grounds to a businessman from Pennsylvania for far less than it was worth. That businessman kept the name, Ruby Pier, and in time, he reopened the park. But it was not ours anymore.

"Emile's spirit was as broken as his body. It took three years before he could walk on his own. We moved away, to a place outside the city, a small flat, where our lives were spent modestly, me tending to my wounded husband and silently nurturing a single wish."

She stopped.

"What wish?" Eddie said.

"That he had never built that place."

The old woman sat in silence. Eddie studied the vast jade sky. He thought about how many times he had wished this same thing, that whoever had built Ruby Pier had done something else with his money.

"I'm sorry about your husband," Eddie said, mostly because he didn't know what else to say.

2 **lathe** [leɪð] **and tar** material that burns easily *(gedrechseltes Holz und Teer)* – 28 **to nurture** *BE:* [ˈnɜːtʃə]; *AE:* [ˈnɜːrtʃər] to keep alive

The old woman smiled. “Thank you, dear. But we lived many years beyond those flames. We raised three children. Emile was sickly, in and out of the hospital. He left me a widow in my fifties. You see this face, these wrinkles?” She turned her cheeks upward. “I earned every one of them.”

Eddie frowned. “I don’t understand. Did we ever... meet? Did you ever come to the pier?”

“No,” she said. “I never wanted to see the pier again. My children went there, and their children and theirs. But not me. My idea of heaven was as far from the ocean as possible, back in that busy diner, when my days were simple, when Emile was courting me.”

Eddie rubbed his temples. When he breathed, mist emerged.

“So why am *I* here?” he said. “I mean, your story, the fire, it all happened before I was born.”

“Things that happen before you are born still affect you,” she said. “And people who come before your time affect you as well.

“We move through places every day that would never have been if not for those who came before us. Our workplaces, where we spend so much time—we often think they began with our arrival. That’s not true.”

She tapped her fingertips together. “If not for Emile, I would have no husband. If not for our marriage, there would be no pier. If there’d been no pier, you would not have ended up working there.”

Eddie scratched his head. “So you’re here to tell me about work?”

“No, dear,” Ruby answered, her voice softening. “I’m here to tell you why your father died.”

The phone call was from Eddie’s mother. His father had collapsed that afternoon, on the east end of the boardwalk near the Junior Rocket Ride. He had a raging fever.

“Eddie, I’m afraid,” his mother said, her voice shaking. She told him of a night, earlier in the week, when his father had come home at dawn, soaking wet. His clothes were full of sand. He was missing a shoe. She said he smelled like the ocean. Eddie bet he smelled like liquor, too.

“He was coughing,” his mother explained. “It just got worse. We should have called a doctor right away... .” She drifted in

13 **mist** a thin fog – 38 **liquor** [ˈlɪkər] *(AE)* strong alcohol

her words. He'd gone to work that day, she said, sick as he was, with his tool belt and his ball peen hammer—same as always—but that night he'd refused to eat and in bed he'd hacked and wheezed and sweated through his undershirt. The next day was worse. And now, this afternoon, he'd collapsed.

"The doctor said it's pneumonia. Oh, I should have done something. I should have *done* something… ."

"What were *you* supposed to do?" Eddie asked. He was mad that she took this on herself. It was his father's drunken fault.

Through the phone, he heard her crying.

Eddie's father used to say he'd spent so many years by the ocean, he breathed seawater. Now, away from that ocean, in the confines of a hospital bed, his body began to wither like a beached fish. Complications developed. Congestion built in his chest. His condition went from fair to stable and from stable to serious. Friends went from saying, "He'll be home in a day," to "He'll be home in a week." In his father's absence, Eddie helped out at the pier, working evenings after his taxi job, greasing the tracks, checking the brake pads, testing the levers, even repairing broken ride parts in the shop.

What he really was doing was protecting his father's job. The owners acknowledged his efforts, then paid him half of what his father earned. He gave the money to his mother, who went to the hospital every day and slept there most nights. Eddie and Marguerite cleaned her apartment and shopped for her food.

When Eddie was a teenager, if he ever complained or seemed bored with the pier, his father would snap, "What? This ain't good enough for you?" And later, when he'd suggested Eddie take a job there after high school, Eddie almost laughed, and his father again said, "What? This ain't good enough for you?" And before Eddie went to war, when he'd talked of marrying Marguerite and becoming an engineer, his father said, "What? This ain't good enough for you?"

And now, despite all that, here he was, at the pier, doing his father's labor.

Finally, one night, at his mother's urging, Eddie visited the hospital. He entered the room slowly. His father, who for years had refused to speak to Eddie, now lacked the strength to even

3 **to hack** to cough violently – 4 **to wheeze** to breathe with difficulty – 6 **pneumonia** *BE:* [njuːˈməʊniə]; *AE:* [nuːˈmoʊnjə] infection of the lungs – 36 **at his mother's urging** because his mother pleaded with him to go

try. He watched his son with heavy-lidded eyes. Eddie, after struggling to find even one sentence to say, did the only thing he could think of to do: He held up his hands and showed his father his grease-stained fingertips.

"Don't sweat it, kid," the other maintenance workers told him. "Your old man will pull through. He's the toughest son of a gun we've ever seen."

Parents rarely let go of their children, so children let go of them. They move on. They move away. The moments that used to define them—a mother's approval, a father's nod—are covered by moments of their own accomplishments. It is not until much later, as the skin sags and the heart weakens, that children understand; their stories, and all their accomplishments, sit atop the stories of their mothers and fathers, stones upon stones, beneath the waters of their lives.

When the news came that his father had died—"slipped away," a nurse told him, as if he had gone out for milk—Eddie felt the emptiest kind of anger, the kind that circles in its cage. Like most workingmen's sons, Eddie had envisioned for his father a heroic death to counter the commonness of his life. There was nothing heroic about a drunken stupor by the beach.

The next day, he went to his parents' apartment, entered their bedroom, and opened all the drawers, as if he might find a piece of his father inside. He rifled through coins, a tie pin, a small bottle of apple brandy, rubber bands, electric bills, pens, and a cigarette lighter with a mermaid on the side. Finally, he found a deck of playing cards. He put it in his pocket.

The funeral was small and brief. In the weeks that followed, Eddie's mother lived in a daze. She spoke to her husband as if he were still there. She yelled at him to turn down the radio. She cooked enough food for two. She fluffed pillows on both sides of the bed, even though only one side had been slept in.

One night, Eddie saw her stacking dishes on the countertop.

"Let me help you," he said.

"No, no," his mother answered, "your father will put them away."

Eddie put a hand on her shoulder.

20 **to counter** to make up for – 21 **drunken stupor** *BE:* ['stju:pə]; *AE:* ['stu:pər] state of semi consciousness due to the consumption of too much alcohol

"Ma," he said, softly. "Dad's gone."

"Gone where?"

The next day, Eddie went to the dispatcher and told him he was quitting. Two weeks later, he and Marguerite moved back into the building where Eddie had grown up, Beachwood Avenue—apartment 6B—where the hallways were narrow and the kitchen window viewed the carousel and where Eddie had accepted a job that would let him keep an eye on his mother, a position he had been groomed for summer after summer: a maintenance man at Ruby Pier. Eddie never said this—not to his wife, not to his mother, not to anyone—but he cursed his father for dying and for trapping him in the very life he'd been trying to escape; a life that, as he heard the old man laughing from the grave, apparently now was good enough for him.

Today Is Eddie's Birthday

He is 37. His breakfast is getting cold.

"You see any salt?" Eddie asks Noel.

Noel, chewing a mouthful of sausage, slides out from the booth, leans across another table, and grabs a salt shaker.

"Here," he mumbles. "Happy birthday."

Eddie shakes it hard. "How tough is it to keep salt on the table?"

"What are you, the manager?" Noel says.

Eddie shrugs. The morning is already hot and thick with humidity. This is their routine: breakfast, once a week, Saturday mornings, before the park gets crazy. Noel works in the dry cleaning business. Eddie helped him get the contract for Ruby Pier's maintenance uniforms.

"What'dya think of this good-lookin' guy?" Noel says. He has a copy of Life *magazine open to a photo of a young political candidate. "How can this guy run for president? He's a kid!"*

Eddie shrugs. "He's about our age."

"No foolin'?" Noel says. He lifts an eyebrow. "I thought you had to be older to be president."

"We are *older," Eddie mumbles.*

Noel closes the magazine. His voice drops. "Hey. You hear what happened at Brighton?"

3 **dispatcher** employee of a transportation company who organizes departures and routes of vehicles

Eddie nods. He sips his coffee. He'd heard. An amusement park. A gondola ride. Something snapped. A mother and her son fell 60 feet to their death.

"You know anybody up there?" Noel asks.

Eddie puts his tongue between his teeth. Every now and then he hears these stories, an accident at a park somewhere, and he shudders as if a wasp just flew by his ear. Not a day passes that he doesn't worry about it happening here, at Ruby Pier, under his watch.

"Nuh-uh," he says. "I don't know no one in Brighton."

He fixes his eyes out the window, as a crowd of beachgoers emerges from the train station. They carry towels, umbrellas, wicker baskets with sandwiches wrapped in paper. Some even have the newest thing: foldable chairs, made from lightweight aluminum.

An old man walks past in a panama hat, smoking a cigar.

"Lookit that guy," Eddie says. "I promise you, he'll drop that cigar on the boardwalk."

"Yeah?" Noel says. "So?"

"It falls in the cracks, then it starts to burn. You can smell it. The chemical they put on the wood. It starts smoking right away. Yesterday I grabbed a kid, couldn't have been more than four years old, about to put a cigar butt in his mouth."

Noel makes a face. "And?"

Eddie turns aside. "And nothing. People should be more careful, that's all."

Noel shovels a forkful of sausage into his mouth. "You're a barrel of laughs. You always this much fun on your birthday?"

Eddie doesn't answer. The old darkness has taken a seat alongside him. He is used to it by now, making room for it the way you make room for a commuter on a crowded bus.

He thinks about the maintenance load today. Broken mirror in the Fun House. New fenders for the bumper cars. Glue, he reminds himself, gotta order more glue. He thinks about those poor people in Brighton. He wonders who's in charge up there.

"What time you finish today?" Noel asks.

Eddie exhales. "It's gonna be busy. Summer. Saturday. You know."

Noel lifts an eyebrow. "We can make the track by six."

7 **to shudder** to shiver from cold or fear – 10 **I don't know no one** *(sl)* I don't know anyone – 17 **Lookit** *(sl)* look at – 34 **gotta** *(sl)* I have got to – 39 **track** a course over which horse races are run

Eddie thinks about Marguerite. He always thinks about Marguerite when Noel mentions the horse track.

"Come on. It's your birthday," Noel says.

Eddie pokes a fork at his eggs, now too cold to bother with.

"All right," he says.

The Third Lesson

"Was the pier so bad?" the old woman asked.

"It wasn't my choice," Eddie said, sighing. "My mother needed help. One thing led to another. Years passed. I never left. I never lived nowhere else. Never made any real money. You know how it is—you get used to something, people rely on you, one day you wake up and you can't tell Tuesday from Thursday. You're doing the same boring stuff, you're a 'ride man,' just like..."

"Your father?"

Eddie said nothing.

"He was hard on you," the old woman said.

Eddie lowered his eyes. "Yeah. So?"

"Perhaps you were hard on him, too."

"I doubt it. You know the last time he talked to me?"

"The last time he tried to strike you."

Eddie shot her a look.

"And you know the last thing he said to me? 'Get a job.' Some father, huh?"

The old woman pursed her lips. "You began to work after that. You picked yourself up."

Eddie felt a rumbling of anger. "Look," he snapped. "You didn't know the guy."

"That's true." She rose. "But I know something you don't. And it is time to show you."

Ruby pointed with the tip of her parasol and drew a circle in the snow. When Eddie looked into the circle, he felt as if his eyes were falling from their sockets and traveling on their own, down a hole and into another moment. The images sharpened. It was years ago, in the old apartment. He could see front and back, above and below.

This is what he saw:

He saw his mother, looking concerned, sitting at the kitchen table. He saw Mickey Shea, sitting across from her. Mickey looked awful. He was soaking wet, and he kept rubbing his hands over his forehead and down his nose. He began to sob. Eddie's mother brought him a glass of water. She motioned for him to wait, and walked to the bedroom and shut the door. She took off her shoes and her housedress. She reached for a blouse and skirt.

Eddie could see all the rooms, but he could not hear what the two of them were saying, it was just blurred noise. He saw Mickey, in the kitchen, ignoring the glass of water, pulling a flask from his jacket and swigging from it. Then, slowly, he got up and staggered to the bedroom. He opened the door.

Eddie saw his mother, half dressed, turn in surprise. Mickey was wobbling. She pulled a robe around her. Mickey came closer. Her hand went out instinctively to block him. Mickey froze, just for an instant, then grabbed that hand and grabbed Eddie's mother and backed her into the wall, leaning against her, grabbing her waist. She squirmed, then yelled, and pushed on Mickey's chest while still gripping her robe. He was bigger and stronger, and he buried his unshaven face below her cheek, smearing tears on her neck.

Then the front door opened and Eddie's father stood there, wet from rain, a ball peen hammer hanging from his belt. He ran into the bedroom and saw Mickey grabbing his wife. Eddie's father hollered. He raised the hammer. Mickey put his hands over his head and charged to the door, knocking Eddie's father sideways. Eddie's mother was crying, her chest heaving, her face streamed with tears. Her husband grabbed her shoulders. He shook her violently. Her robe fell. They were both screaming. Then Eddie's father left the apartment, smashing a lamp with the hammer on his way out. He thumped down the steps and ran off into the rainy night.

"What was that?" Eddie yelled in disbelief. "What the hell was *THAT*?"

The old woman held her tongue. She stepped to the side of the snowy circle and drew another one. Eddie tried not to look down. He couldn't help it. He was falling again, becoming eyes at a scene.

This is what he saw:

2 **to sob** to cry / weep quietly (sobbing is the noise rather than the action) *(schluchzen)* – 13 **robe** here: a dress – 17 **to squirm** [skwɜːm] to twist and wriggle in order to set yourself free – 34 **to hold your tongue** to be quiet, not say anything

He saw a rainstorm at the farthest edge of Ruby Pier—the "north point," they called it—a narrow jetty that stretched far out into the ocean. The sky was a bluish black. The rain was falling in sheets. Mickey Shea came stumbling toward the edge of the jetty. He fell to the ground, his stomach heaving in and out. He lay there for a moment, face to the darkened sky, then rolled on his side, under the wood railing. He dropped into the sea.

Eddie's father appeared moments later, scrambling back and forth, the hammer still in his hand. He grabbed the railing, searching the waters. The wind blew the rain in sideways. His clothes were drenched and his leather tool belt was nearly black from the soaking. He saw something in the waves. He stopped, pulled off the belt, yanked off one shoe, tried to undo the other, gave up, squatted under the railing and jumped, splashing clumsily in the churning ocean.

Mickey was bobbing in the insistent roll of seawater, half unconscious, a foamy yellow fluid coming from his mouth. Eddie's father swam to him, yelling into the wind. He grabbed Mickey. Mickey swung. Eddie's father swung back. The skies clapped with thunder as the rainwater pelted them. They grabbed and flailed in the violent chop.

Mickey coughed hard as Eddie's father grabbed his arm and hooked it over his shoulder. He went under, came up again, then braced his weight against Mickey's body, pointing them toward shore. He kicked. They moved forward. A wave swept them back. Then forward again. The ocean thumped and crashed, but Eddie's father remained wedged under Mickey's armpit, pumping his legs, blinking wildly to clear his vision.

They caught the crest of a wave and made sudden progress shoreward. Mickey moaned and gasped. Eddie's father spit out seawater. It seemed to take forever, the rain popping, the white foam smacking their faces, the two men grunting, thrashing their arms. Finally, a high, curling wave lifted them up and dumped them onto the sand, and Eddie's father rolled out from under Mickey and was able to hook his hands under Mickey's arms and hold him from being swept into the surf. When the waves receded, he yanked Mickey forward with a final surge, then collapsed on the shore, his mouth open, filling with wet sand.

2 **jetty** a seawall that extends into the water to prevent the beach from being washed away – 21 **as the rainwater pelted them** as rain poured heavily down on them

Eddie's vision returned to his body. He felt exhausted, spent, as if he had been in that ocean himself. His head was heavy. Everything he thought he'd known about his father, he didn't seem to know anymore.

"What was he *doing*?" Eddie whispered.

"Saving a friend," Ruby said.

Eddie glared at her. "Some friend. If I'd have known what he did, I'd have let his drunken hide drown."

"Your father thought about that, too," the old woman said. "He had chased after Mickey to hurt him, perhaps even to kill him. But in the end, he couldn't. He knew who Mickey was. He knew his shortcomings. He knew he drank. He knew his judgment faltered.

"But many years earlier, when your father was looking for work, it was Mickey who went to the pier owner and vouched for him. And when you were born, it was Mickey who lent your parents what little money he had, to help pay for the extra mouth to feed. Your father took old friendships seriously—"

"Hold on, lady," Eddie snapped. "Did you see what that bastard was doing with my mother?"

"I did," the old woman said sadly. "It was wrong. But things are not always what they seem.

"Mickey had been fired that afternoon. He'd slept through another shift, too drunk to wake up, and his employers told him that was enough. He handled the news as he handled all bad news, by drinking more, and he was thick with whiskey by the time he reached your mother. He was begging for help. He wanted his job back. Your father was working late. Your mother was going to take Mickey to him.

"Mickey was coarse, but he was not evil. At that moment, he was lost, adrift, and what he did was an act of loneliness and desperation. He acted on impulse. A bad impulse. Your father acted on impulse, too, and while his first impulse was to kill, his final impulse was to keep a man alive."

She crossed her hands over the end of her parasol.

"That was how he took ill, of course. He lay there on the beach for hours, soaking and exhausted, before he had the strength to struggle home. Your father was no longer a young man. He was already in his fifties."

12 **shortcoming** weakness in a person's character – 13 **to falter** to be weak or unsure – 15 **to vouch for sb** to recommend sb, say that they are honest or to be trusted – 30 **coarse** lacking good manners, vulgar

"Fifty-six," Eddie said blankly.

"Fifty-six," the old woman repeated. "His body had been weakened, the ocean had left him vulnerable, pneumonia took hold of him, and in time, he died."

"Because of Mickey?" Eddie said.

"Because of loyalty," she said.

"People don't die because of loyalty."

"They don't?" She smiled. "Religion? Government? Are we not loyal to such things, sometimes to the death?"

Eddie shrugged.

"Better," she said, "to be loyal to one another."

After that, the two of them remained in the snowy mountain valley for a long time. At least to Eddie it felt long. He wasn't sure how long things took anymore.

"What happened to Mickey Shea?" Eddie said.

"He died, alone, a few years later," the old woman said. "Drank his way to the grave. He never forgave himself for what happened."

"But my old man," Eddie said, rubbing his forehead. "He never said anything."

"He never spoke of that night again, not to your mother, not to anyone else. He was ashamed for her, for Mickey, for himself. In the hospital, he stopped speaking altogether. Silence was his escape, but silence is rarely a refuge. His thoughts still haunted him.

"One night his breathing slowed and his eyes closed and he could not be awakened. The doctors said he had fallen into a coma."

Eddie remembered that night. Another phone call to Mr. Nathanson. Another knock on his door.

"After that, your mother stayed by his bedside. Days and nights. She would moan to herself, softly, as if she were praying: 'I should have done something. I should have done something… .'

"Finally, one night, at the doctors' urging, she went home to sleep. Early the next morning, a nurse found your father slumped halfway out the window."

"Wait," Eddie said. His eyes narrowed. "The window?"

Ruby nodded. "Sometime during the night, your father awakened. He rose from his bed, staggered across the room, and found the strength to raise the window sash. He called your mother's name with what little voice he had, and he called yours, too, and your brother, Joe. And he called for Mickey. At that moment, it seemed, his heart was spilling out, all the guilt and regret. Perhaps he felt the light of death approaching. Perhaps he only knew you were all out there somewhere, in the streets beneath his window. He bent over the ledge. The night was chilly. The wind and damp, in his state, were too much. He was dead before dawn.

"The nurses who found him dragged him back to his bed. They were frightened for their jobs, so they never breathed a word. The story was he died in his sleep."

Eddie fell back, stunned. He thought about that final image. His father, the tough old war horse, trying to crawl out a window. Where was he going? What was he thinking? Which was worse when left unexplained: a life, or a death?

"How do you know all this?" Eddie asked Ruby.

She sighed. "Your father lacked the money for a hospital room of his own. So did the man on the other side of the curtain."

She paused.

"Emile. My husband."

Eddie lifted his eyes. His head moved back as if he'd just solved a puzzle.

"Then you *saw* my father."

"Yes."

"And my mother."

"I heard her moaning on those lonely nights. We never spoke. But after your father's death, I inquired about your family. When I learned where he had worked, I felt a stinging pain, as if I had lost a loved one myself. The pier that bore my name. I felt its cursed shadow, and I wished again that it had never been built.

"That wish followed me to heaven, even as I waited for you."

Eddie looked confused.

"The diner?" she said. She pointed to the speck of light in the mountains. "It's there because I wanted to return to my younger years, a simple but secure life. And I wanted all those who had ever suffered at Ruby Pier—every accident, every fire, every fight, slip, and fall—to be safe and secure. I wanted them all like I wanted my Emile, warm, well fed, in the cradle of a welcoming place, far from the sea."

1 **sash** frame – 8 **chilly** cold

Ruby stood, and Eddie stood, too. He could not stop thinking about his father's death.

"I hated him," he mumbled.

The old woman nodded.

"He was hell on me as a kid. And he was worse when I got older."

Ruby stepped toward him. "Edward," she said softly. It was the first time she had called him by name. "Learn this from me. Holding anger is a poison. It eats you from inside. We think that hating is a weapon that attacks the person who harmed us. But hatred is a curved blade. And the harm we do, we do to ourselves.

"Forgive, Edward. Forgive. Do you remember the lightness you felt when you first arrived in heaven?"

Eddie did. *Where is my pain?*

"That's because no one is born with anger. And when we die, the soul is freed of it. But now, here, in order to move on, you must understand why you felt what you did, and why you no longer need to feel it."

She touched his hand.

"You need to forgive your father."

Eddie thought about the years that followed his father's funeral. How he never achieved anything, how he never went anywhere. For all that time, Eddie had imagined a certain life—a "could have been" life—that would have been his if not for his father's death and his mother's subsequent collapse. Over the years, he glorified that imaginary life and held his father accountable for all of its losses: the loss of freedom, the loss of career, the loss of hope. He never rose above the dirty, tiresome work his father had left behind.

"When he died," Eddie said, "he took part of me with him. I was stuck after that."

Ruby shook her head. "Your father is not the reason you never left the pier."

Eddie looked up. "Then what is?"

She patted her skirt. She adjusted her spectacles. She began to walk away. "There are still two people for you to meet," she said.

11 **blade** the flat part of a knife with a cutting edge – 27 **to hold sb accountable for sth** to blame sb for sth

Eddie tried to say "Wait," but a cold wind nearly ripped the voice from his throat. Then everything went black.

Ruby was gone. He was back atop the mountain, outside the diner, standing in the snow.

He stood there for a long time, alone in the silence, until he realized the old woman was not coming back. Then he turned to the door and slowly pulled it open. He heard clanking silverware and dishes being stacked. He smelled freshly cooked food—breads and meats and sauces. The spirits of those who had perished at the pier were all around, engaged with one another, eating and drinking and talking.

Eddie moved haltingly, knowing what he was there to do. He turned to his right, to the corner booth, to the ghost of his father, smoking a cigar. He felt a shiver. He thought about the old man hanging out that hospital window, dying alone in the middle of the night.

"Dad?" Eddie whispered.

His father could not hear him. Eddie drew closer. "Dad. I know what happened now."

He felt a choke in his chest. He dropped to his knees alongside the booth. His father was so close that Eddie could see the whiskers on his face and the frayed end of his cigar. He saw the baggy lines beneath his tired eyes, the bent nose, the bony knuckles and squared shoulders of a workingman. He looked at his own arms and realized, in his earthly body, he was now older than his father. He had outlived him in every way.

"I was angry with you, Dad. I hated you."

Eddie felt tears welling. He felt a shaking in his chest. Something was flushing out of him.

"You beat me. You shut me out. I didn't understand. I still don't understand. Why did you do it? Why?" He drew in long painful breaths. "I didn't know, OK? I didn't know your life, what happened. I didn't *know* you. But you're my father. I'll let it go now, all right? All right? Can we let it go?"

His voice wobbled until it was high and wailing, not his own anymore. "OK? YOU HEAR ME?" he screamed. Then softer: "You hear me? Dad?"

He leaned in close. He saw his father's dirty hands. He spoke the last familiar words in a whisper.

12 **haltingly** slowly, starting and stopping, hesitatingly – 36 **to wobble** to shake, to tremble

"It's fixed."

Eddie pounded the table, then slumped to the floor. When he looked up, he saw Ruby standing across the way, young and beautiful. She dipped her head, opened the door, and lifted off into the jade sky.

THURSDAY, 11 A.M.

Who would pay for Eddie's funeral? He had no relatives. He'd left no instructions. His body remained at the city morgue, as did his clothes and personal effects, his maintenance shirt, his socks and shoes, his linen cap, his wedding ring, his cigarettes and pipe cleaners, all awaiting claim.

In the end, Mr. Bullock, the park owner, footed the bill, using the money he saved from Eddie's no-longer-cashable paycheck. The casket was a wooden box. The church was chosen by location—the one nearest the pier—as most attendees had to get back to work.

A few minutes before the service, the pastor asked Dominguez, wearing a navy blue sport coat and his good black jeans, to step inside his office.

"Could you share some of the deceased's unique qualities?" the pastor asked. "I understand you worked with him."

Dominguez swallowed. He was none too comfortable with clergymen. He hooked his fingers together earnestly, as if giving the matter some thought, and spoke as softly as he thought one should speak in such a situation.

"Eddie," he finally said, "really loved his wife."

He unhooked his fingers, then quickly added, "Of course, I never met her."

11 **to foot the bill** to pay the bill

The Fourth Person Eddie Meets in Heaven

Eddie blinked, and found himself in a small, round room. The mountains were gone and so was the jade sky. A low plaster ceiling just missed his head. The room was brown—as plain as shipping wrap—and empty, save for a wooden stool and an oval mirror on the wall.

Eddie stepped in front of the mirror. He cast no reflection. He saw only the reverse of the room, which expanded suddenly to include a row of doors. Eddie turned around.

Then he coughed.

The sound startled him, as if it came from someone else. He coughed again, a hard, rumbling cough, as if things needed to be resettled in his chest.

When did *this* start? Eddie thought. He touched his skin, which had aged since his time with Ruby. It felt thinner now, and drier. His midsection, which during his time with the Captain had felt tight as pulled rubber, was loose with flab, the droop of age.

There are still two people for you to meet, Ruby had said. And then what? His lower back had a dull ache. His bad leg was growing stiffer. He realized what was happening, it happened with each new stage of heaven. He was rotting away.

He approached one of the doors and pushed it open. Suddenly, he was outside, in the yard of a home he had never seen, in a land that he did not recognize, in the midst of what appeared to be a wedding reception. Guests holding silver plates filled the grassy lawn. At one end stood an archway covered in red flowers and birch branches, and at the other end, next to Eddie, stood the door that he had walked through. The bride, young and pretty, was in the center of the group, removing a pin from her butter-colored hair. The groom was lanky. He wore a black wedding coat and held up a sword, and at the hilt of the sword was a ring. He lowered it toward the bride and guests cheered as she took it. Eddie heard their voices, but the language was foreign. German? Swedish?

He coughed again. The group looked up. Every person seemed to smile, and the smiling frightened Eddie. He backed quickly through the door from which he'd entered, figuring to return

16 **flab** fat – 25 **wedding reception** a formal party after a wedding

to the round room. Instead, he was in the middle of another wedding, indoors this time, in a large hall, where the people looked Spanish and the bride wore orange blossoms in her hair. She was dancing from one partner to the next, and each guest handed her a small sack of coins.

Eddie coughed again—he couldn't help it—and when several of the guests looked up, he backed through the door and again entered a different wedding scene, something African, Eddie guessed, where families poured wine onto the ground and the couple held hands and jumped over a broom. Then another pass through the door to a Chinese reception, where firecrackers were lit before cheering attendees, then another doorway to something else—maybe French?—where the couple drank together from a two-handled cup.

How long does this go on? Eddie thought. In each reception, there were no signs of how the people had gotten there, no cars or buses, no wagons, no horses. Departure did not appear to be an issue. The guests milled about, and Eddie was absorbed as one of them, smiled at but never spoken to, much like the handful of weddings he had gone to on earth. He preferred it that way. Weddings were, in Eddie's mind, too full of embarrassing moments, like when couples were asked to join in a dance, or to help lift the bride in a chair. His bad leg seemed to glow at those moments, and he felt as if people could see it from across the room.

Because of that, Eddie avoided most receptions, and when he did go, he often stood in the parking lot, smoking a cigarette, waiting for time to pass. For a long stretch, there were no weddings to attend, anyhow. Only in the late years of his life, when some of his teenaged pier workers had grown up and taken spouses, did he find himself getting the faded suit out of the closet and putting on the collared shirt that pinched his thick neck. By this point, his once-fractured leg bones were spurred and deformed. Arthritis had invaded his knee. He limped badly and was thus excused from all participatory moments, such as dances or candle lightings. He was considered an "old man," alone, unattached, and no one expected him to do much besides smile when the photographer came to the table.

Here, now, in his maintenance clothes, he moved from one wedding to the next, one reception to another, one language, one cake, and one type of music to another language, another cake, and another type of music. The uniformity did not surprise Eddie. He always figured a wedding here was not much different from a wedding there. What he didn't get was what this had to do with *him.*

He pushed through the threshold one more time and found himself in what appeared to be an Italian village. There were vineyards on the hillsides and farmhouses of travertine stone. Many of the men had thick, black hair, combed back and wet, and the women had dark eyes and sharp features. Eddie found a place against a wall and watched the bride and groom cut a log in half with a two-handed rip saw. Music played—flutists, violinists, guitarists—and guests began the tarantella, dancing in a wild, twirling rhythm. Eddie took a few steps back. His eyes wandered to the edge of the crowd.

A bridesmaid in a long lavender dress and a stitched straw hat moved through the guests, with a basket of candy-covered almonds. From afar, she looked to be in her 20s.

"Per l'amaro e il dolce?" she said, offering her sweets. "*Per l'amaro e il dolce? ... Per l'amaro e il dolce?...*"

At the sound of her voice, Eddie's whole body shook. He began to sweat. Something told him to run, but something else froze his feet to the ground. She came his way. Her eyes found him from beneath the hat brim, which was topped with parchment flowers.

"Per l'amaro e il dolce?" she said, smiling, holding out the almonds. "For the bitter and the sweet?"

Her dark hair fell over one eye and Eddie's heart nearly burst. His lips took a moment to part, and the sound from the back of his throat took a moment to rise, but they came together in the first letter of the only name that ever made him feel this way. He dropped to his knees.

"Marguerite..." he whispered.

"For the bitter and the sweet," she said.

Today Is Eddie's Birthday

Eddie and his brother are sitting in the maintenance shop.

"This," Joe says proudly, holding up a drill, "is the newest model."

9 **log** large piece of the branch or trunk of a tree – 9 **rip saw** a tool for cutting wood *(Spaltsäge)* – 21 **parchment flowers** artificial flowers made of very thin paper *(Pergament)*

Joe is wearing a checkered sport coat and black-and-white saddle shoes. Eddie thinks his brother looks too fancy—and fancy means phony—but Joe is a salesman for a hardware company now and Eddie has been wearing the same outfit for years, so what does he know?

"Yes, sir," Joe says, "and get this. It runs on that battery."

Eddie holds the battery between his fingers, a small thing called nickel cadmium. Hard to believe.

"Start it up," Joe says, handing the drill over.

Eddie squeezes the trigger. It explodes in noise.

"Nice, huh?" Joe yells.

That morning, Joe had told Eddie his new salary. It was three times what Eddie made. Then Joe had congratulated Eddie on his promotion: head of maintenance for Ruby Pier, his father's old position. Eddie had wanted to answer, "If it's so great, why don't you take it, and I'll take your job?" But he didn't. Eddie never said anything he felt that deeply.

"Helloo? Anybody in here?"

Marguerite is at the door, holding a reel of orange tickets. Eddie's eyes go, as always, to her face, her olive skin, her dark coffee eyes. She has taken a job in the ticket booths this summer and she wears the official Ruby Pier uniform: a white shirt, a red vest, black stirrup pants, a red beret, and her name on a pin below her collarbone. The sight of it makes Eddie angry—especially in front of his hotshot brother.

"Show her the drill," Joe says. He turns to Marguerite. "It's battery operated."

Eddie squeezes. Marguerite grabs her ears.

"It's louder than your snoring," she says.

"Whoa-ho!" Joe yells, laughing. "Whoa-ho! She got you!"

Eddie looks down sheepishly, then sees his wife smiling.

"Can you come outside?" she says.

Eddie waves the drill. "I'm working here."

"Just for a minute, OK?"

Eddie stands up slowly, then follows her out the door. The sun hits his face.

"HAP-PY BIRTH-DAY, MR. ED-DIE!" *a group of children scream in unison.*

"Well, I'll be," Eddie says.

Marguerite yells, "OK, kids, put the candles on the cake!"

3 **phony** false, pretending to be what one is not

The children race to a vanilla sheet cake sitting on a nearby folding table. Marguerite leans toward Eddie and whispers, "I promised them you'd blow out all thirty-eight at once."

Eddie snorts. He watches his wife organize the group. As always with Marguerite and children, his mood is lifted by her easy connection to them and dampened by her inability to bear them. One doctor said she was too nervous. Another said she had waited too long, she should have had them by age 25. In time, they ran out of money for doctors. It was what it was.

For nearly a year now, she has been talking about adoption. She went to the library. She brought home papers. Eddie said they were too old. She said, "What's too old to a child?"

Eddie said he'd think about it.

"All right," she yells now from the sheet cake. "Come on, Mr. Eddie! Blow them out. Oh, wait, wait..." She fishes in a bag and pulls out a camera, a complicated contraption with rods and tabs and a round flashbulb.

"Charlene let me use it. It's a Polaroid."

Marguerite lines up the picture, Eddie over the cake, the children squeezing in around him, admiring the 38 little flames. One kid pokes Eddie and says, "Blow them all out, OK?"

Eddie looks down. The frosting is a mess, full of countless little handprints.

"I will," Eddie says, but he is looking at his wife.

EDDIE STARED AT the young Marguerite.

"It's not you," he said.

She lowered her almond basket. She smiled sadly. The tarantella was dancing behind them and the sun was fading behind a ribbon of white clouds.

"It's not you," Eddie said again.

The dancers yelled, *"Hooheyy!"* They banged tambourines.

She offered her hand. Eddie reached for it quickly, instinctively, as if grabbing for a falling object. Their fingers met and he had never felt such a sensation, as if flesh were forming over his own flesh, soft and warm and almost ticklish. She knelt down beside him.

"It's not you," he said.

"It *is* me," she whispered.

Hooheyy!

14 **sheet cake** flat cake (*here:* Eddie's birthday cake) – 35 **ticklish** *kitzlig*

"It's not you, it's not you, it's not you," Eddie mumbled, as he dropped his head onto her shoulder and, for the first time since his death, began to cry.

Their own wedding took place Christmas Eve on the second floor of a dimly lit Chinese restaurant called Sammy Hong's. The owner, Sammy, agreed to rent it for that night, figuring he'd have little other business. Eddie took what cash he had left from the army and spent it on the reception—roast chicken and Chinese vegetables and port wine and a man with an accordion. The chairs for the ceremony were needed for the dinner, so once the vows were taken, the waiters asked the guests to rise, then carried the chairs downstairs to the tables. The accordion man sat on a stool. Years later, Marguerite would joke that the only thing missing from their wedding "were the bingo cards."

When the meal was finished and some small gifts were given, a final toast was offered and the accordion man packed his case. Eddie and Marguerite left through the front door. It was raining lightly, a chilly rain, but the bride and groom walked home together, seeing as it was only a few blocks. Marguerite wore her wedding dress beneath a thick pink sweater. Eddie wore his white suit coat, the shirt pinching his neck. They held hands. They moved through pools of lamplight. Everything around them seemed buttoned up tight.

People say they "find" love, as if it were an object hidden by a rock. But love takes many forms, and it is never the same for any man and woman. What people find then is a *certain* love. And Eddie found a certain love with Marguerite, a grateful love, a deep but quiet love, one that he knew, above all else, was irreplaceable. Once she'd gone, he'd let the days go stale. He put his heart to sleep.

Now, here she was again, as young as the day they were wed.

"Walk with me," she said.

Eddie tried to stand, but his bad knee buckled. She lifted him effortlessly.

"Your leg," she said, regarding the faded scar with a tender familiarity. Then she looked up and touched the tufts of hair above his ears.

"It's white," she said, smiling.

19 **seeing as it was** because it was – 29 **stale** [steɪl] *here:* uninteresting, cold

Eddie couldn't get his tongue to move. He couldn't do much but stare. She was exactly as he remembered—more beautiful, really, for his final memories of her had been as an older, suffering woman. He stood beside her, silent, until her dark eyes narrowed and her lips crept up mischievously.

"Eddie." She almost giggled. "Have you forgotten so fast how I used to look?"

Eddie swallowed. "I never forgot that."

She touched his face lightly and the warmth spread through his body. She motioned to the village and the dancing guests.

"All weddings," she said, happily. "That was my choice. A world of weddings, behind every door. Oh, Eddie, it never changes, when the groom lifts the veil, when the bride accepts the ring, the possibilities you see in their eyes, it's the same around the world. They truly believe their love and their marriage is going to break all the records."

She smiled. "Do you think we had that?"

Eddie didn't know how to answer.

"We had an accordion player," he said.

They walked from the reception and up a gravel path. The music faded to a background noise. Eddie wanted to tell her everything he had seen, everything that had happened. He wanted to ask her about every little thing and every big thing, too. He felt a churning inside him, a stop-start anxiety. He had no idea where to begin.

"You did this, too?" he finally said. "You met five people?"

She nodded.

"A different five people," he said.

She nodded again.

"And they explained everything? And it made a difference?"

She smiled. "All the difference." She touched his chin. "And then I waited for you."

He studied her eyes. Her smile. He wondered if her waiting had felt like his.

"How much do you know... about me? I mean, how much do you know since..."

He still had trouble saying it.

"Since you died."

She removed the straw hat and pushed the thick, young locks away from her forehead. "Well, I know everything that happened when we were together... ."

She pursed her lips.

"And now I know *why* it happened... ."

She put her hands on her chest.

"And I also know... that you loved me dearly."

She took his other hand then. He felt the melting warmth.

"I don't know how *you* died," she said.

Eddie thought for a moment.

"I'm not sure, either," he said. "There was a girl, a little girl, she wandered into this ride, and she was in trouble... ."

Marguerite's gaze widened. She looked so young. This was harder than Eddie figured, telling his wife about the day he was killed.

"They have these rides, see, these new rides, nothing like what we used to have—everyone has to go a thousand miles an hour now. Anyhow, this one ride, it drops these carts, and the hydraulics are supposed to stop it, bring it down slowly, but something sliced the cable, the cart snapped loose, I still can't figure it, but the cart dropped because I told them to release it—I mean, I told Dom, he's this kid who works with me now—it wasn't his fault—but I told him and then I tried to stop it, but he couldn't hear me, and this little girl was just sitting there, and I tried to reach her. I tried to save her. I felt her little hands, but then I..."

He stopped. She tilted her head, urging him to go on. He exhaled deeply.

"I ain't talked this much since I got here," he said.

She nodded and smiled, a gentle smile, and at the sight of it, his eyes began to moisten and a wave of sadness washed over him and suddenly, just like that, none of this mattered, nothing about his death or the park or the crowd he had yelled at to "Get back!" Why was he talking about this? What was he doing? Was he really with *her*? Like a hidden grieving that rises to grab the heart, his soul was ambushed with old emotions, and his lips began to tremble and he was swept into the current of all that he had lost. He was looking at his wife, his dead wife, his young wife, his missing wife, his only wife, and he didn't want to look anymore.

"Oh God, Marguerite," he whispered. "I'm so sorry, I'm so sorry. I can't say. I can't say. I can't say."

He dropped his head into his hands and he said it anyhow, he said what everyone says.

"I missed you so much."

Today Is Eddie's Birthday

The racetrack is crowded with summer customers. The women wear straw sunhats and the men smoke cigars. Eddie and Noel leave work early to play Eddie's birthday number, 39, in the Daily Double. They sit on slatted fold-down seats. At their feet are paper cups of beer, amidst a carpet of discarded tickets.

Earlier, Eddie won the first race of the day. He'd put half of those winnings on the second race and won that as well, the first time such a thing had ever happened to him. That gave him $209. After losing twice in smaller bets, he put it all on a horse to win in the sixth, because, as he and Noel agreed, in exuberant logic, he'd arrived with next to nothing, so what harm done if he went home the same way?

"Just think, if you win," Noel says now, "you'll have all that dough for the kid."

The bell rings. The horses are off. They bunch together on the far straightaway, their colorful silks blurring with their bumpy movement. Eddie has No. 8, a horse named Jersey Finch, which isn't a bad gamble, not at four to one, but what Noel has just said about "the kid"—the one Eddie and Marguerite are planning to adopt—flushes him with guilt. They could have used that money. Why did he do things like this?

The crowd rises. The horses come down the stretch. Jersey Finch moves outside and lengthens into full stride. The cheering mixes with the thundering hooves. Noel hollers. Eddie squeezes his ticket. He is more nervous than he wants to be. His skin goes bumpy. One horse pulls ahead of the pack.

Jersey Finch!

Now Eddie has nearly $800.

"I gotta call home," he says.

"You'll ruin it," Noel says.

"What are you talking about?"

"You tell somebody, you ruin your luck."

"You're nuts."

"Don't do it."

"I'm calling her. It'll make her happy."

"It won't make her happy."

4 **slatted** with slats (slats are thin pieces of wood; so the seats of the chairs have holes in them) – 14 **dough** [dəʊ] *(AE, sl)* money – 16 **straightaway** the part of the race track which is straight, not a bend – 33 **nuts** *(sl)* mad

He limps to a pay phone and drops in a nickel. Marguerite answers. Eddie tells her the news. Noel is right. She is not happy. She tells him to come home. He tells her to stop telling him what to do.

"We have a baby coming," she scolds. "You can't keep behaving like this."

Eddie hangs up the phone with a heat behind his ears. He goes back to Noel, who is eating peanuts at the railing.

"Let me guess," Noel says.

They go to the window and pick another horse. Eddie takes the money from his pocket. Half of him doesn't want it anymore and half of him wants twice as much, so he can throw it on the bed when he gets home and tell his wife, "Here, buy whatever you want, OK?"

Noel watches him push the bills through the opening. He raises his eyebrows.

"I know, I know," Eddie says.

What he does not know is that Marguerite, unable to call him back, has chosen to drive to the track and find him. She feels badly about yelling, this being his birthday, and she wants to apologize; she also wants him to stop. She knows from evenings past that Noel will insist they stay until closing—Noel is like that. And since the track is only ten minutes away, she grabs her handbag and drives their secondhand Nash Rambler down Ocean Parkway. She turns right on Lester Street. The sun is gone and the sky is in flux. Most of the cars are coming from the other direction. She approaches the Lester Street overpass, which used to be how customers reached the track, up the stairs, over the street and back down the stairs again, until the track owners paid the city for a traffic light, which left the overpass, for the most part, deserted.

But on this night, it is not deserted. It holds two teenagers who do not want to be found, two 17-year-olds who, hours earlier, had been chased from a liquor store after stealing five cartons of cigarettes and three pints of Old Harper's whiskey. Now, having finished the alcohol and smoked many of the cigarettes, they are bored with the evening, and they dangle their empty bottles over the lip of the rusted railing.

"Dare me?" one says.

"Dare ya," says the other.

26 **the sky is in flux** the sky is changing, i.e. it is dusk (nearly night) – 39 **to dare** to suggest to sb to do sth dangerous

The first one lets the bottle drop and they duck behind the metal grate to watch. It just misses a car and shatters onto the pavement.

"Whoooo," the second one yells. "Did you see that!"

"Drop yours now, chicken."

The second one stands, holds out his bottle, and chooses the sparse traffic of the right-hand lane. He wiggles the bottle back and forth, trying to time the drop to land between vehicles, as if this was some sort of art and he was some sort of artist.

His fingers release. He almost smiles.

Forty feet below, Marguerite never thinks to look up, never thinks that anything might be happening on that overpass, never thinks about anything besides getting Eddie out of that racetrack while he still has some money left. She is wondering what section of the grandstand to look in, even as the Old Harper's whiskey bottle smashes her windshield into a spray of flying glass. Her car veers into the concrete divider. Her body is tossed like a doll, slamming against the door and the dashboard and the steering wheel, lacerating her liver and breaking her arm and thumping her head so hard she loses touch with the sounds of the evening. She does not hear the screeching of cars. She does not hear the honking of horns. She does not hear the retreat of rubber-soled sneakers, running down the Lester Street overpass and off into the night.

LOVE, LIKE RAIN, can nourish from above, drenching couples with a soaking joy. But sometimes, under the angry heat of life, love dries on the surface and must nourish from below, tending to its roots, keeping itself alive.

The accident on Lester Street sent Marguerite to the hospital. She was confined to bed rest for nearly six months. Her injured liver recovered eventually, but the expense and the delay cost them the adoption. The child they were expecting went to someone else. The unspoken blame for this never found a resting place—it simply moved like a shadow from husband to wife. Marguerite went quiet for a long time. Eddie lost himself in work. The shadow took a place at their table and they ate in its presence, amid the lonely clanking of forks and plates. When they spoke, they spoke of small things. The water of their love was hidden beneath the roots. Eddie never bet the horses again.

17 **concrete divider** wall of concrete *(Beton)* that separates the two lanes of a road – 19 **to lacerate** to cut in a violent way

His visits with Noel came to a gradual end, each of them unable to discuss much over breakfast that didn't feel like an effort.

An amusement park in California introduced the first tubular steel tracks—they twisted at severe angles unachievable with wood—and suddenly, roller coasters, which had faded to near oblivion, were back in fashion. Mr. Bullock, the park owner, had ordered a steel-track model for Ruby Pier, and Eddie oversaw the construction. He barked at the installers, checking their every move. He didn't trust anything this fast. Sixty-degree angles? He was sure someone would get hurt. Anyhow, it gave him a distraction.

The Stardust Band Shell was torn down. So was the Zipper ride. And the Tunnel of Love, which kids found too corny now. A few years later, a new boat ride called a log flume was constructed, and, to Eddie's surprise, it was hugely popular. The riders floated through troughs of water and dropped, at the end, into a large splash pool. Eddie couldn't figure why people so loved getting wet, when the ocean was 300 yards away. But he maintained it just the same, working shoeless in the water, ensuring that the boats never loosened from the tracks.

In time, husband and wife began talking again, and one night, Eddie even spoke about adopting. Marguerite rubbed her forehead and said, "We're too old now."

Eddie said, "What's too old to a child?"

The years passed. And while a child never came, their wound slowly healed, and their companionship rose to fill the space they were saving for another. In the mornings, she made him toast and coffee, and he dropped her at her cleaning job then drove back to the pier. Sometimes, in the afternoons, she got off early and walked the boardwalk with him, following his rounds, riding carousel horses or yellow-painted clamshells as Eddie explained the rotors and cables and listened for the engines' hum.

One July evening, they found themselves walking by the ocean, eating grape popsicles, their bare feet sinking in the wet sand. They looked around and realized they were the oldest people on the beach.

Marguerite said something about the bikini bathing suits the young girls were wearing and how she would never have the nerve to wear such a thing. Eddie said the girls were lucky,

5 **to fade to near oblivion** to be nearly forgotten – 31 **clamshell** shell-shaped, open "cars" in a carousel which people ride in – 35 **popsicle** ice lolly

because if she did the men would not look at anyone else. And even though by this point Marguerite was in her mid-40s and her hips had thickened and a web of small lines had formed around her eyes, she thanked Eddie gratefully and looked at his crooked nose and wide jaw. The waters of their love fell again from above and soaked them as surely as the sea that gathered at their feet.

Three years later, she was breading chicken cutlets in the kitchen of their apartment, the one they had kept all this time, long after Eddie's mother had died, because Marguerite said it reminded her of when they were kids, and she liked to see the old carousel out the window. Suddenly, without warning, the fingers of her right hand stretched open uncontrollably. They moved backward. They would not close. The cutlet slid from her palm. It fell into the sink. Her arm throbbed. Her breathing quickened. She stared for a moment at this hand with the locked fingers that appeared to belong to someone else, someone gripping a large, invisible jar.

Then everything went dizzy.

"Eddie?" she called, but by the time he arrived, she had passed out on the floor.

It was, they would determine, a tumor on the brain, and her decline would be like many others, treatments that made the disease seem mild, hair falling out in patches, mornings spent with noisy radiation machines and evenings spent vomiting in a hospital toilet.

In the final days, when cancer was ruled the victor, the doctors said only, "Rest. Take it easy." When she asked questions, they nodded sympathetically, as if their nods were medicine doled out with a dropper. She realized this was protocol, their way of being nice while being helpless, and when one of them suggested "getting your affairs in order," she asked to be released from the hospital. She told more than asked.

Eddie helped her up the stairs and hung her coat as she looked around the apartment. She wanted to cook but he made her sit, and he heated some water for tea. He had purchased lamb chops the day before, and that night he bumbled through a dinner with several invited friends and coworkers, most of whom greeted Marguerite and her sallow complexion with sentences

39 **sallow** unhealthy – 39 **complexion** colour and texture of the skin of the face

like, "Well, look who's back!" as if this were a homecoming and not a farewell party.

They ate mashed potatoes from a CorningWare dish and had butterscotch brownies for dessert, and when Marguerite finished a second glass of wine, Eddie took the bottle and poured her a third.

Two days later, she awoke with a scream. He drove her to the hospital in the predawn silence. They spoke in short sentences, what doctor might be on, who Eddie should call. And even though she was sitting in the seat next to him, Eddie felt her in everything, in the steering wheel, in the gas pedal, in the blinking of his eye, in the clearing of his throat. Every move he made was about hanging on to her.

She was 47.

"You have the card?" she asked him.

"The card… " he said blankly.

She drew a deep breath and closed her eyes, and her voice was thinner when she resumed speaking, as if that breath had cost her dearly.

"Insurance," she croaked.

"Yeah, yeah," he said quickly. "I got the card."

They parked in the lot and Eddie shut the engine. It was suddenly too still and too quiet. He heard every tiny sound, the squeak of his body on the leather seat, the *ca-cunk* of the door handle, the rush of outside air, his feet on the pavement, the jangle of his keys.

He opened her door and helped her get out. Her shoulders were scrunched up near her jaws, like a freezing child. Her hair blew across her face. She sniffed and lifted her eyes to the horizon. She motioned to Eddie and nodded toward the distant top of a big, white amusement ride, with red carts dangling like tree ornaments.

"You can see it from here," she said.

"The Ferris wheel?" he said.

She looked away. "Home."

Because he had not slept in heaven, it was Eddie's perception that he had not spent more than a few hours with any of the people he'd met. Then again, without night or day, without sleeping or waking, without sunsets or high tides or meals or schedules, how did he know?

With Marguerite, he wanted only time—more and more time—and he was granted it, nighttimes and daytimes and nighttimes again. They walked through the doors of the assorted weddings and spoke of everything he wished to speak about. At a Swedish ceremony, Eddie told her about his brother, Joe, who had died 10 years earlier from a heart attack, just a month after purchasing a new condominium in Florida. At a Russian ceremony, she asked if he had kept the old apartment, and he said that he had, and she said she was glad. At an outdoor ceremony in a Lebanese village, he spoke about what had happened to him here in heaven, and she seemed to listen and know at the same time. He spoke of the Blue Man and his story, why some die when others live, and he spoke about the Captain and his tale of sacrifice. When he spoke about his father, Marguerite recalled the many nights he had spent enraged at the man, confounded by his silence. Eddie told her he had made things square, and her eyebrows lifted and her lips spread and Eddie felt an old, warm feeling he had missed for years, the simple act of making his wife happy.

One night, Eddie spoke about the changes at Ruby Pier, how the old rides had been torn down, how the pennywhistle music at the arcade was now blaring rock 'n' roll, how the roller coasters now had corkscrew twists and carts that hung *down* from the tracks, how the "dark" rides, which once meant cowboy cutouts in glow paint, were full of video screens now, like watching television all the time.

He told her the new names. No more Dippers or Tumble Bugs. Everything was the Blizzard, the Mindbender, Top Gun, the Vortex.

"Sounds strange, don't it?" Eddie said.

"It sounds," she said, wistfully, "like someone else's summer."

Eddie realized that was precisely what he'd been feeling for years.

"I should have worked somewhere else," he told her. "I'm sorry I never got us out of there. My dad. My leg. I always felt like such a bum after the war."

He saw a sadness pass over her face.

"What happened?" she asked. "During that war?"

He had never quite told her. It was all understood. Soldiers, in his day, did what they had to do and didn't speak of it once they

5 **condominium** *(AE)* one apartment in a block of many apartments – 13 **confounded** confused, perplexed – 14 **to make things square** to settle an argument – 26 **bug** *(AE)* insect – 29 **wistful** full of longing and sadness

came home. He thought about the men he'd killed. He thought about the guards. He thought about the blood on his hands. He wondered if he'd ever be forgiven.

"I lost myself," he said.

"No," his wife said.

"Yes," he whispered, and she said nothing else.

At times, there in heaven, the two of them would lie down together. But they did not sleep. On earth, Marguerite said, when you fell asleep, you sometimes dreamed your heaven and those dreams helped to form it. But there was no reason for such dreams now.

Instead, Eddie held her shoulders and nuzzled in her hair and took long, deep breaths. At one point, he asked his wife if God knew he was here. She smiled and said, "Of course," even when Eddie admitted that some of his life he'd spent hiding from God, and the rest of the time he thought he went unnoticed.

The Fourth Lesson

Finally, after many talks, Marguerite walked Eddie through another door. They were back inside the small, round room. She sat on the stool and placed her fingers together. She turned to the mirror, and Eddie noticed her reflection. Hers, but not his.

"The bride waits here," she said, running her hands along her hair, taking in her image but seeming to drift away. "This is the moment you think about what you're doing. Who you're choosing. Who you will love. If it's right, Eddie, this can be such a wonderful moment."

She turned to him.

"You had to live without love for many years, didn't you?"

Eddie said nothing.

"You felt that it was snatched away, that I left you too soon."

He lowered himself slowly. Her lavender dress was spread before him.

"You *did* leave too soon," he said.

"You were angry with me."

"No."

Her eyes flashed.

"OK. Yes."

"There was a reason to it all," she said.

"What reason?" he said. "How could there be a reason? You died. You were forty-seven. You were the best person any of us knew, and you died and you lost everything. And I lost everything. I lost the only woman I ever loved."

She took his hands. "No, you didn't. I was right here. And you loved me anyway.

"Lost love is still love, Eddie. It takes a different form, that's all. You can't see their smile or bring them food or tousle their hair or move them around a dance floor. But when those senses weaken, another heightens. Memory. Memory becomes your partner. You nurture it. You hold it. You dance with it.

"Life has to end," she said. "Love doesn't."

Eddie thought about the years after he buried his wife. It was like looking over a fence. He was aware of another kind of life out there, even as he knew he would never be a part of it.

"I never wanted anyone else," he said quietly.

"I know," she said.

"I was still in love with you."

"I know." She nodded. "I felt it."

"Here?" he asked.

"Even here," she said, smiling. "That's how strong lost love can be."

She stood and opened a door, and Eddie blinked as he entered behind her. It was a dimly lit room, with foldable chairs, and an accordion player sitting in the corner.

"I was saving this one," she said.

She held out her arms. And for the first time in heaven, he initiated his contact, he came to her, ignoring the leg, ignoring all the ugly associations he had made about dance and music and weddings, realizing now that they were really about loneliness.

"All that's missing," Marguerite whispered, taking his shoulder, "is the bingo cards."

He grinned and put a hand behind her waist.

"Can I ask you something?" he said.

"Yes."

"How come you look the way you looked the day I married you?"

"I thought you'd like it that way."

He thought for a moment. "Can you change it?"

"Change it?" She looked amused. "To what?"

"To the end."

24 **dimly lit** with only few sources of light

She lowered her arms. "I wasn't so pretty at the end."

Eddie shook his head, as if to say not true.

"Could you?"

She took a moment, then came again into his arms. The accordion man played the familiar notes. She hummed in his ear and they began to move together, slowly, in a remembered rhythm that a husband shares only with his wife.

You made me love you
I didn't want to do it
I didn't want to do it...
You made me love you
and all the time you knew it
and all the time you knew it. ...

When he moved his head back, she was 47 again, the web of lines beside her eyes, the thinner hair, the looser skin beneath her chin. She smiled and he smiled, and she was, to him, as beautiful as ever, and he closed his eyes and said for the first time what he'd been feeling from the moment he saw her again: "I don't want to go on. I want to stay here."

When he opened his eyes, his arms still held her shape, but she was gone, and so was everything else.

FRIDAY, 3.15 p.m.

Dominguez pressed the elevator button and the door rumbled closed. An inner porthole lined up with an exterior porthole. The car jerked upward, and through the meshed glass he watched the lobby disappear.

"I can't believe this elevator still works," Dominguez said. "It must be, like, from the last century."

The man beside him, an estate attorney, nodded slightly, feigning interest. He took off his hat—it was stuffy, and he was sweating—and watched the numbers light up on the brass panel. This was his third appointment of the day. One more, and he could go home to dinner.

"Eddie didn't have much," Dominguez said.

28 **estate attorney** [ətɜːni] lawyer who administrates the affairs of people that have died *(Nachlassverwalter)*

"Um-hmm," the man said, wiping his forehead with a handkerchief. "Then it shouldn't take long."

The elevator bounced to a stop and the door rumbled open and they turned toward 6B. The hallway still had the black-and-white checkered tile of the 1960s, and it smelled of someone's cooking—garlic and fried potatoes. The superintendent had given them the key—along with a deadline. Next Wednesday. Have the place cleared out for a new tenant.

"Wow..." Dominguez said, upon opening the door and entering the kitchen. "Pretty tidy for an old guy." The sink was clean. The counters were wiped. Lord knows, he thought, *his* place was never this neat.

"Financial papers?" the man asked. "Bank statements? Jewelry?"

Dominguez thought of Eddie wearing jewelry and he almost laughed. He realized how much he missed the old man, how strange it was not having him at the pier, barking orders, watching everything like a mother hawk. They hadn't even cleared out his locker. No one had the heart. They just left his stuff at the shop, where it was, as if he were coming back tomorrow.

"I dunno. You check in that bedroom thing?"

"The bureau?"

"Yeah. You know, I only been here once myself. I really only knew Eddie through work."

Dominguez leaned over the table and glanced out the kitchen window. He saw the old carousel. He looked at his watch. *Speaking of work*, he thought to himself.

The attorney opened the top drawer of the bedroom bureau. He pushed aside the pairs of socks, neatly rolled, one inside the other, and the underwear, white boxer shorts, stacked by the waistbands. Tucked beneath them was an old leather-bound box, a serious-looking thing. He flipped it open in hopes of a quick find. He frowned. Nothing important. No bank statements. No insurance policies. Just a black bow tie, a Chinese restaurant menu, an old deck of cards, a letter with an army medal, and a faded Polaroid of a man by a birthday cake, surrounded by children.

"Hey," Dominguez called from the other room, "is this what you need?"

He emerged with a stack of envelopes taken from a kitchen drawer, some from a local bank, some from the Veterans

21 **dunno** *(sl)* don't know

Administration. The attorney fingered through them and, without looking up, said, "That'll do." He pulled out one bank statement and made a mental note of the balance. Then, as often happened with these visits, he silently congratulated himself on his own portfolio of stocks, bonds, and a vested retirement plan. It sure beat ending up like this poor slob, with little to show but a tidy kitchen.

The Fifth Person Eddie Meets in Heaven

White. There was only white now. No earth, no sky, no horizon between the two. Only a pure and silent white, as noiseless as the deepest snowfall at the quietest sunrise.

White was all Eddie saw. All he heard was his own labored breathing, followed by an echo of that breathing. He inhaled and heard a louder inhale. He exhaled, and it exhaled, too.

Eddie squeezed his eyes shut. Silence is worse when you know it won't be broken, and Eddie knew. His wife was gone. He wanted her desperately, one more minute, half a minute, five more seconds, but there was no way to reach or call or wave or even look at her picture. He felt as if he'd tumbled down steps and was crumpled at the bottom. His soul was vacant. He had no impulse. He hung limp and lifeless in the void, as if on a hook, as if all the fluids had been gored out of him. He might have hung there a day or a month. It might have been a century.

Only at the arrival of a small but haunting noise did he stir, his eyelids lifting heavily. He had already been to four pockets of heaven, met four people, and while each had been mystifying upon arrival, he sensed that this was something altogether different.

The tremor of noise came again, louder now, and Eddie, in a lifelong defense instinct, clenched his fists, only to find his right hand squeezing a cane. His forearms were pocked with liver spots. His fingernails were small and yellowish. His bare legs carried the reddish rash—shingles—that had come during his final weeks on earth. He looked away from his hastening decay. In human accounting, his body was near its end.

Now came the sound again, a high-pitched rolling of irregular shrieks and lulls. In life, Eddie had heard this sound in his nightmares, and he shuddered with the memory: the village,

6 **slob** *(sl)* lazy, useless person – 20 **void** empty space

the fire, Smitty and this noise, this squealing cackle that, in the end, emerged from his own throat when he tried to speak.

He clenched his teeth, as if that might make it stop, but it continued on, like an unheeded alarm, until Eddie yelled into the choking whiteness: "What is it? *What do you want?*"

With that, the high-pitched noise moved to the background, layered atop a second noise, a loose, relentless rumble—the sound of a running river—and the whiteness shrank to a sun spot reflecting off shimmering waters. Ground appeared beneath Eddie's feet. His cane touched something solid. He was high up on an embankment, where a breeze blew across his face and a mist brought his skin to a moist glaze. He looked down and saw, in the river, the source of those haunting screeches, and he was flushed with the relief of a man who finds, while gripping the baseball bat, that there is no intruder in his house. The sound, this screaming, whistling, thrumming screak, was merely the cacophony of children's voices, thousands of them at play, splashing in the river and shrieking with innocent laughter.

Was this what I'd been dreaming? he thought. *All this time? Why?* He studied the small bodies, some jumping, some wading, some carrying buckets while others rolled in the high grass. He noticed a certain calmness to it all, no roughhousing, which you usually saw with kids. He noticed something else. There were no adults. Not even teenagers. These were all small children, with skin the color of dark wood, seemingly monitoring themselves.

And then Eddie's eyes were drawn to a white boulder. A slender young girl stood upon it, apart from the others, facing his direction. She motioned with both her hands, waving him in. He hesitated. She smiled. She waved again and nodded, as if to say, *Yes, you.*

Eddie lowered his cane to navigate the downward slope. He slipped, his bad knee buckling, his legs giving way. But before he hit the earth, he felt a sudden blast of wind at his back and he was whipped forward and straightened on his feet, and there he was, standing before the little girl as if he'd been there all the time.

11 **embankment** sloping land beside a river or lake, bank – 22 **roughhousing** energetic, sometimes dangerous playing

Today Is Eddie's Birthday

He is 51. A Saturday. It is his first birthday without Marguerite. He makes Sanka in a paper cup, and eats two pieces of toast with margarine. In the years after his wife's accident, Eddie shooed away any birthday celebrations, saying, "Why do I gotta be reminded of that day for?" It was Marguerite who insisted. She made the cake. She invited friends. She always purchased one bag of taffy and tied it with a ribbon. "You can't give away your birthday," she would say.

Now that she's gone, Eddie tries. At work, he straps himself on a roller coaster curve, high and alone, like a mountain climber. At night, he watches television in the apartment. He goes to bed early. No cake. No guests. It is never hard to act ordinary if you feel ordinary, and the paleness of surrender becomes the color of Eddie's days.

He is 60, a Wednesday. He gets to the shop early. He opens a brown-bag lunch and rips a piece of bologna off a sandwich. He attaches it to a hook, then drops the twine down the fishing hole. He watches it float. Eventually, it disappears, swallowed by the sea.

He is 68, a Saturday. He spreads his pills on the counter. The telephone rings. Joe, his brother, is calling from Florida. Joe wishes him happy birthday. Joe talks about his grandson. Joe talks about a condominium. Eddie says "uh-huh" at least 50 times.

*He is 75, a Monday. He puts on his glasses and checks the maintenance reports. He notices someone missed a shift the night before and the Squiggly Wiggly Worm Adventure has not been brake-tested. He sighs and takes a placard from the wall—*RIDE CLOSED TEMPORARILY FOR MAINTENANCE*—then carries it across the boardwalk to the Wiggly Worm entrance, where he checks the brake panel himself.*

He is 82, a Tuesday. A taxi arrives at the park entrance. He slides inside the front seat, pulling his cane in behind him.

"Most people like the back," the driver says.

"You mind?" Eddie asks.

The driver shrugs. "Nah. I don't mind." Eddie looks straight ahead. He doesn't say that it feels more like driving this way, and he hasn't driven since they refused him a license two years ago.

2 **Sanka** (brand name) instant coffee – 4 **Why do I gotta be...?** *(sl)* Why have I got to be...?

The taxi takes him to the cemetery. He visits his mother's grave and his brother's grave and he stands by his father's grave for only a few moments. As usual, he saves his wife's for last. He leans on the cane and he looks at the headstone and he thinks about many things. Taffy. He thinks about taffy. He thinks it would take his teeth out now, but he would eat it anyhow, if it meant eating it with her.

The Last Lesson

The little girl appeared to be Asian, maybe five or six years old, with a beautiful cinnamon complexion, hair the color of a dark plum, a small flat nose, full lips that spread joyfully over her gapped teeth, and the most arresting eyes, as black as a seal's hide, with a pinhead of white serving as a pupil. She smiled and flapped her hands excitedly until Eddie edged one step closer, whereupon she presented herself.

"Tala," she said, offering her name, her palms on her chest.

"Tala," Eddie repeated.

She smiled as if a game had begun. She pointed to her embroidered blouse, loosely slung over her shoulders and wet with the river water.

"*Baro,*" she said.

"Baro."

She touched the woven red fabric that wrapped around her torso and legs.

"*Saya.*"

"Saya."

Then came her cloglike shoes—"*bakya*"—then the iridescent seashells by her feet—"*capiz*"—then a woven bamboo mat—"*banig*"—that was laid out before her. She motioned for Eddie to sit on the mat and she sat, too, her legs curled underneath her.

None of the other children seemed to notice him. They splashed and rolled and collected stones from the river's floor. Eddie watched one boy rub a stone over the body of another, down his back, under his arms.

"Washing," the girl said. "Like our *inas* used to do."

"Inas?" Eddie said.

She studied Eddie's face.

9 **cinnamon** a sweet, light brown, light brown spice *(Zimt)* – 12 **hide** (animal's) skin

"Mommies," she said.

Eddie had heard many children in his life, but in this one's voice, he detected none of the normal hesitation toward adults. He wondered if she and the other children had chosen this riverbank heaven, or if, given their short memories, such a serene landscape had been chosen for them.

She pointed to Eddie's shirt pocket. He looked down. Pipe cleaners.

"These?" he said. He pulled them out and twisted them together, as he had done in his days at the pier. She rose to her knees to examine the process. His hands shook. "You see? It's a..." he finished the last twist ". . . dog."

She took it and smiled—a smile Eddie had seen a thousand times.

"You like that?" he said.

"You burn me," she said.

Eddie felt his jaw tighten.

"What did you say?"

"You burn me. You make me fire."

Her voice was flat, like a child reciting a lesson.

"My ina say to wait inside the *nipa*. My ina say to hide."

Eddie lowered his voice, his words slow and deliberate.

"What... were you hiding *from*, little girl?"

She fingered the pipe-cleaner dog, then dipped it in the water.

"*Sundalong*," she said.

"Sundalong?"

She looked up.

"Soldier."

Eddie felt the word like a knife in his tongue. Images flashed through his head. Soldiers. Explosions. Morton. Smitty. The Captain. The flamethrowers.

"Tala..." he whispered.

"Tala," she said, smiling at her own name.

"Why are you here, in heaven?"

She lowered the animal.

"You burn me. You make me fire."

Eddie felt a pounding behind his eyes. His head began to rush. His breathing quickened.

"You were in the Philippines... the shadow... in that hut..."

6 **serene** *BE:* [sɪˈriːn]; *AE:* [səˈriːn] peaceful and calm

"The *nipa*. Ina say be safe there. Wait for her. Be safe. Then big noise. Big fire. You burn me." She shrugged her narrow shoulders. "Not safe."

Eddie swallowed. His hands trembled. He looked into her deep, black eyes and he tried to smile, as if it were a medicine the little girl needed. She smiled back, but this only made him fall apart. His face collapsed, and he buried it in his palms. His shoulders and lungs gave way. The darkness that had shadowed him all those years was revealing itself at last, it was real, flesh and blood, this child, this lovely child, he had killed her, burned her to death, the bad dreams he'd suffered, he'd deserved every one. He *had* seen something! That shadow in the flame! Death by his hand! *By his own fiery hand!* A flood of tears soaked through his fingers and his soul seemed to plummet.

He wailed then, and a howl rose within him in a voice he had never heard before, a howl from the very belly of his being, a howl that rumbled the river water and shook the misty air of heaven. His body convulsed, and his head jerked wildly, until the howling gave way to prayerlike utterances, every word expelled in the breathless surge of confession: "I killed you, I KILLED YOU," then a whispered "forgive me," then, "FORGIVE ME, OH, GOD..." and finally, "What have I done... *WHAT HAVE I DONE?* ..."

He wept and he wept, until the weeping drained him to a shiver. Then he shook silently, swaying back and forth. He was kneeling on a mat before the little dark-haired girl, who played with her pipe-cleaner animal along the bank of the flowing river.

At some point, when his anguish had quieted, Eddie felt a tapping on his shoulder. He looked up to see Tala holding out a stone.

"You wash me," she said. She stepped into the water and turned her back to Eddie. Then she pulled the embroidered baro over her head.

He recoiled. Her skin was horribly burned. Her torso and narrow shoulders were black and charred and blistered. When she turned around, the beautiful, innocent face was covered in grotesque scars. Her lips drooped. Only one eye was open. Her

7 **to fall apart** here: to break down – 14 **to plummet** to fall down rapidly – 18 **to convulse** to shake violently – 29 **anguish** extreme distress – 35 **to recoil** to move back with surprise

hair was gone in patches of burned scalp, covered now by hard, mottled scabs.

"You wash me," she said again, holding out the stone.

Eddie dragged himself into the river. He took the stone. His fingers trembled.

"I don't know how…" he mumbled, barely audible. "I never had children… ."

She raised her charred hand and Eddie gripped it gently and slowly rubbed the stone along her forearm, until the scars began to loosen. He rubbed harder; they peeled away. He quickened his efforts until the singed flesh fell and the healthy flesh was visible. Then he turned the stone over and rubbed her bony back and tiny shoulders and the nape of her neck and finally her cheeks and her forehead and the skin behind her ears.

She leaned backward into him, resting her head on his collarbone, shutting her eyes as if falling into a nap. He traced gently around the lids. He did the same with her drooped lips, and the scabbed patches on her head, until the plum-colored hair emerged from the roots and the face that he had seen at first was before him again.

When she opened her eyes, their whites flashed out like beacons. "I am five," she whispered.

Eddie lowered the stone and shuddered in short, gasping breaths. "Five... uh-huh... Five years old?..."

She shook her head no. She held up five fingers. Then she pushed them against Eddie's chest, as if to say *your* five. *Your fifth person.*

A warm breeze blew. A tear rolled down Eddie's face. Tala studied it the way a child studies a bug in the grass. Then she spoke to the space between them.

"Why sad?" she said.

"Why am I sad?" he whispered. "Here?"

She pointed down. "There."

Eddie sobbed, a final vacant sob, as if his chest were empty. He had surrendered all barriers; there was no grown-up-to-child talk anymore. He said what he always said, to Marguerite, to Ruby, to the Captain, to the Blue Man, and, more than anyone, to himself.

11 **singed** lightly burned – 18 **scabbed patches** areas of skin with a crustlike surface covering a healing wound

"I was sad because I didn't do anything with my life. I was nothing. I accomplished nothing. I was lost. I felt like I wasn't supposed to be there."

Tala plucked the pipe-cleaner dog from the water.

"Supposed to be there," she said.

"Where? At Ruby Pier?"

She nodded.

"Fixing rides? That was my existence?" He blew a deep breath. "Why?"

She tilted her head, as if it were obvious.

"Children," she said. "You keep them safe. You make good for me."

She wiggled the dog against his shirt.

"Is where you were supposed to be," she said, and then she touched his shirt patch with a small laugh and added two words, "Eddie Main-ten-ance."

Eddie slumped in the rushing water. The stones of his stories were all around him now, beneath the surface, one touching another. He could feel his form melting, dissolving, and he sensed that he did not have long, that whatever came after the five people you meet in heaven, it was upon him now.

"Tala?" he whispered.

She looked up.

"The little girl at the pier? Do you know about her?"

Tala stared at her fingertips. She nodded yes.

"Did I save her? Did I pull her out of the way?"

Tala shook her head. "No pull."

Eddie shivered. His head dropped. So there it was. The end of his story.

"Push," Tala said.

He looked up. "Push?"

"Push her legs. No pull. You push. Big thing fall. You keep her safe."

Eddie shut his eyes in denial. "But I felt her hands," he said. "It's the only thing I remember. I *couldn't* have pushed her. I felt her *hands*."

Tala smiled and scooped up river water, then placed her small wet fingers in Eddie's adult grip. He knew right away they had been there before.

2 **to accomplish** *BE:* [ə'kʌmplɪʃ]; *AE:* [ə'kɑ:mplɪʃ] **sth** to achieve sth

"Not *her* hands," she said. "*My* hands. I bring you to heaven. Keep you safe."

With that, the river rose quickly, engulfing Eddie's waist and chest and shoulders. Before he could take another breath, the noise of the children disappeared above him, and he was submerged in a strong but silent current. His grip was still entwined with Tala's, but he felt his body being washed from his soul, meat from the bone, and with it went all the pain and weariness he ever held inside him, every scar, every wound, every bad memory.

He was nothing now, a leaf in the water, and she pulled him gently, through shadow and light, through shades of blue and ivory and lemon and black, and he realized all these colors, all along, were the emotions of his life. She drew him up through the breaking waves of a great gray ocean and he emerged in brilliant light above an almost unimaginable scene:

There was a pier filled with thousands of people, men and women, fathers and mothers and children—so many children—children from the past and the present, children who had not yet been born, side by side, hand in hand, in caps, in short pants, filling the boardwalk and the rides and the wooden platforms, sitting on each other's shoulders, sitting in each other's laps. They were there, or would be there, because of the simple, mundane things Eddie had done in his life, the accidents he had prevented, the rides he had kept safe, the unnoticed turns he had affected every day. And while their lips did not move, Eddie heard their voices, more voices than he could have imagined, and a peace came upon him that he had never known before. He was free of Tala's grasp now, and he floated up above the sand and above the boardwalk, above the tent tops and spires of the midway, toward the peak of the big, white Ferris wheel, where a cart, gently swaying, held a woman in a yellow dress—his wife, Marguerite, waiting with her arms extended. He reached for her and he saw her smile and the voices melded into a single word from God:

Home.

3 **to engulf** to flow over – 24 **mundane** ordinary

Epilogue

The park at Ruby Pier reopened three days after the accident. The story of Eddie's death was in the newspapers for a week, and then other stories about other deaths took its place.

The ride called Freddy's Free Fall was closed for the season, but the next year it reopened with a new name, Daredevil Drop. Teenagers saw it as a badge of courage, and it drew many customers, and the owners were pleased.

Eddie's apartment, the one he had grown up in, was rented to someone new, who put leaded glass in the kitchen window, obscuring the view of the old carousel. Dominguez, who had agreed to take over Eddie's job, put Eddie's few possessions in a trunk at the maintenance shop, alongside memorabilia from Ruby Pier, including photos of the original entrance.

Nicky, the young man whose key had cut the cable, made a new key when he got home, then sold his car four months later. He returned often to Ruby Pier, where he bragged to his friends that his great-grandmother was the woman for whom it was named.

Seasons came and seasons went. And when school let out and the days grew long, the crowds returned to the amusement park by the great gray ocean—not as large as those at the theme parks, but large enough. Come the summer, the spirit turns, and the seashore beckons with a song of the waves, and people gather for carousels and Ferris wheels and sweet iced drinks and cotton candy.

Lines formed at Ruby Pier—just as a line formed someplace else: five people, waiting, in five chosen memories, for a little girl named Amy or Annie to grow and to love and to age and to die, and to finally have her questions answered—why she lived and what she lived for. And in that line now was a whiskered old man, with a linen cap and a crooked nose, who waited in a place called the Stardust Band Shell to share his part of the secret of heaven: that each affects the other and the other affects the next, and the world is full of stories, but the stories are all one.

16 **to brag** to show off

Acknowledgments

The author wishes to thank Vinnie Curci, of Amusements of America, and Dana Wyatt, director of operations for Pacific Park on the Santa Monica Pier. Their assistance in researching this book was invaluable, and their pride in protecting fun park customers is laudable. Also, thanks to Dr. David Collon, of Henry Ford Hospital, for the information on war wounds. And Kerri Alexander, who handles, well, everything. My deepest appreciation to Bob Miller, Ellen Archer, Will Schwalbe, Leslie Wells, Jane Comins, Katie Long, Michael Burkin, and Phil Rose for their inspiring belief in me; to David Black, for what agent-author relationships should be; to Janine, who patiently heard this book read aloud, many times; to Rhoda, Ira, Cara, and Peter, with whom I shared my first Ferris wheel; and to my uncle, the real Eddie, who told me his stories long before I told my own.

The Japanese Empire in 1942

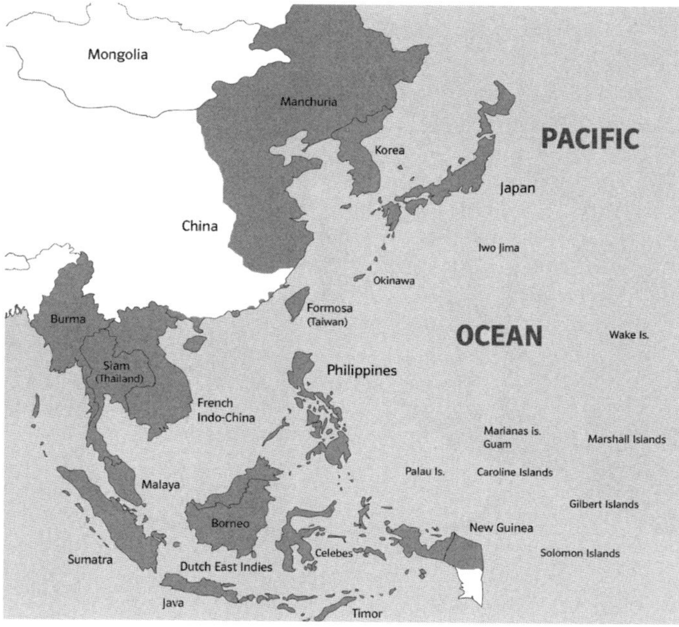

The Japanese military forces quickly took advantage of their success at Pearl Harbor to expand their presence and power eastwards throughout the Pacific and westwards towards India. There was almost no resistance to this program of aggressive expansion until mid-1942. Then, after losing the Battle of Midway, Japan was slowly forced to retreat and began losing island after island to the Allied Forces. This rapid change of fortune was a surprise even to the American military.

Three Reviews of *The Five People You Meet in Heaven*

1. David M. Kusumoto (San Diego, CA United States) (Review found at Amazon.com)

The Five People You Meet in Heaven is remarkable in its simplicity, and it has all the basic story telling elements down that makes for a good read. I really believe it's the kind of title that will never go out of print. People will still be talking about it fifty years from now. And it will forever polarize readers.

I think it's too easy for people, some guilty of overt intellectual snobbery, to scoff at works like *The Five People You Meet in Heaven* at the exclusion and denigration of all that is mainstream and "popular," as if the masses who made this book a success are all wrong and they themselves are sure-headed and right.

Just don't believe them. *The Five People You Meet in Heaven* is for you if you find other thick and weighty titles a little daunting after a while. It's the perfect break, a refreshing change of pace for a guy like me used to going through so many books that feel like work, titles filled with depressing themes and sentences as tortuous in construction as they are in their efforts to provide messages that are pseudo-revelatory and profound.

I like books for the "masses" just as much as I like prize-winning titles stretching several hundred pages each, some good, some great and some awful. And *The Five People You Meet in Heaven* isn't designed to please critics. It's unfair and just plain mean-spirited to accuse any author of "making money" or "selling out" when it's obvious that he/she has tapped into something that resonates and brings optimism to many people who might otherwise avoid books. There's nothing wrong, in my view, with reaching out to as many people as possible and giving them hope and contentment amidst the turbulence of their everyday lives.

8 **overt** obvious, open – 10 **denigration** expressing disapproval of something – 14 **daunting** discouraging – 19 **pseudo-revalatory** pretending to reveal a truth or an insight, but not really doing so – 29 **amidst** in

2. A. G. Popa Lisseanu "anapopa" (Review found at Amazon.com)

I cannot understand the good critics I have read about this book. I don't like to leave books unfinished, but when I had reached the second person that Eddie meets in heaven, I could not read one more word... I find this book terribly boring, easy and unrefined, bad literature, that doesn't know how to transmit feelings. Moreover it is supposed to be a lesson of morality, but it is such an empty morality. Does not inspire me at all. I definitely do not recommend this book to people who like real, good literature.

3. (For Heaven's Sake - A Review by Sacha Zimmerman. From The New Republic Online, June 17 2004)

Truthfully, I don't believe in heaven — I have no clue as to what, if anything, comes next, whether it's Valhalla, Nirvana, the Garden of Eden, reincarnation, or absolutely nothing. My fundamental problem with the concept is that it acts as some kind of celestial incentive to be a good person on Earth. But there are plenty of Earthly and tangible reasons to do so already. If I tend to an elderly relative, it is because I care for that relative's well-being and quality of life, not because I desire a reward. And, frankly, that's a much more profound way to live in the world: behaving for the sake of doing what's right, not for the sake of gain.

...But actually America loves Albom and his hokey ways; *The Five People You Meet In Heaven* was on The New York Times' best-seller list for over 36 weeks. It's easy to feel an affinity for this simplistic, folksy bathos; it's easier, after all, to act for the sake of heaven than to make the considered and nuanced moral choices that really confront us in life. And it is here that Albom fails. His character makes no moral choices, he does not ponder the depths of his existence, he is merely a reactive stick figure that has to go to cotton-candy heaven to learn that his life had meaning. It's single-serve religion for a drive-thru, strip-mall, mega-church kind of country.

13 **celestial** heavenly – 14 **incentive** motivator – 20 **hokey** *(sl)* sentimental, soppy, phoney – 23 **bathos** triviality – 29 **strip-mall** open area shopping centre with shops arranged in a row and a sidewalk in front